The Struggle for Time and Space Begins Aga[in]

DVD VIDEO

D0339516

Pokémon Trainer Ash and his Pikachu must find the Jewel of Life and stop Arceus from devastating all existence! The journey will be both dangerous and uncertain: even if Ash and his friends can set an old wrong right again, will there be time to return the Jewel of Life before Arceus destroys everything and everyone they've ever known?

Manga adaptation also available from VIZ Media

POKÉMON
ARCEUS
JEWEL OF LIFE
A TALE UNTOLD: A LEGEND UNLEASHED

POKÉMON
ARCEUS
AND THE
JEWEL OF LIFE

RATED A FOR ALL AGES
ratings.viz.com

www.vizkids.com

media
www.viz.com

2011 Pokémon. © 1997-2009 Nintendo, Creatures, GAME FREAK, TV Tokyo, ShoPro, JR Kikaku. © Pikachu Project 2009. Pokémon properties are trademarks of Nintendo.

More Adventures COMING SOON...

Tep and Gigi get along so well together... But something is about to change! How will this affect their relationship?!

VOL. 6 AVAILABLE MARCH 2012!

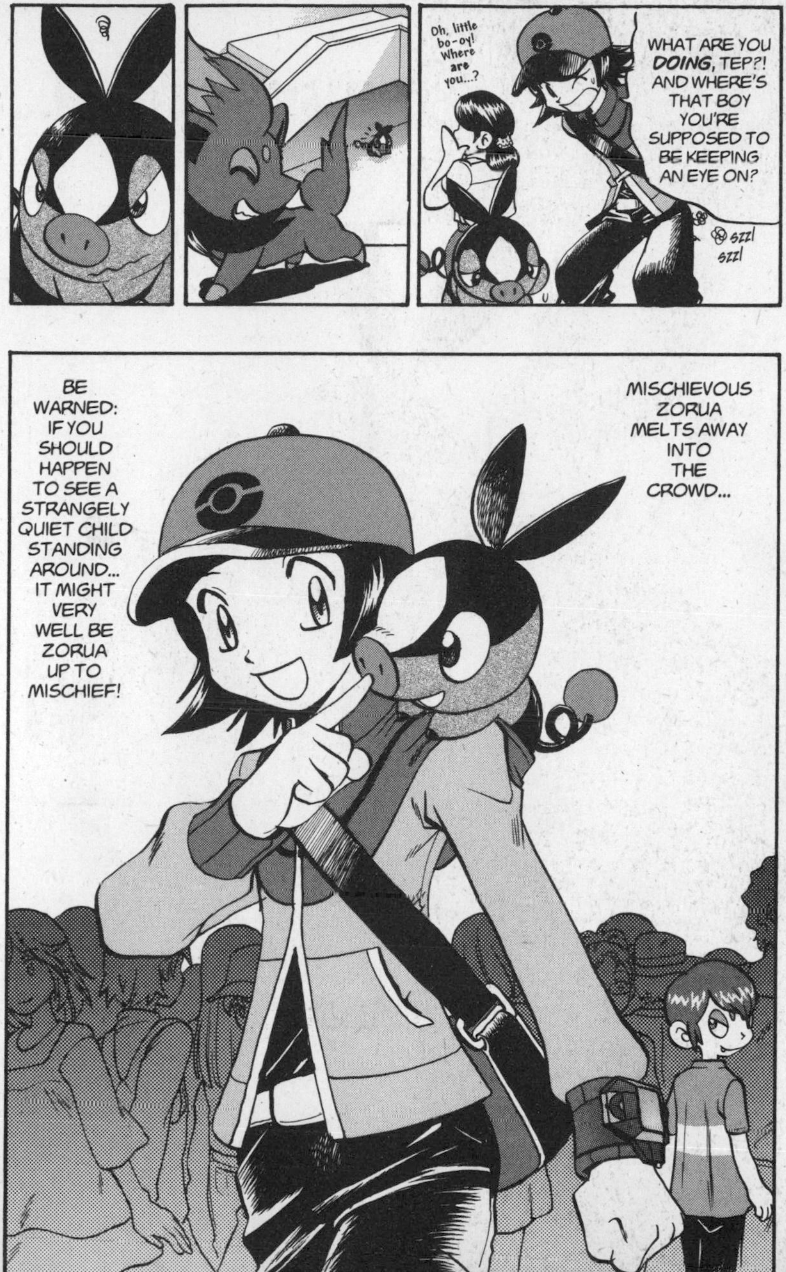
Oh, little bo-oy! Where are you...?
WHAT ARE YOU DOING, TEP?! AND WHERE'S THAT BOY YOU'RE SUPPOSED TO BE KEEPING AN EYE ON?
szzl szzl
BE WARNED: IF YOU SHOULD HAPPEN TO SEE A STRANGELY QUIET CHILD STANDING AROUND... IT MIGHT VERY WELL BE ZORUA UP TO MISCHIEF!
MISCHIEVOUS ZORUA MELTS AWAY INTO THE CROWD...

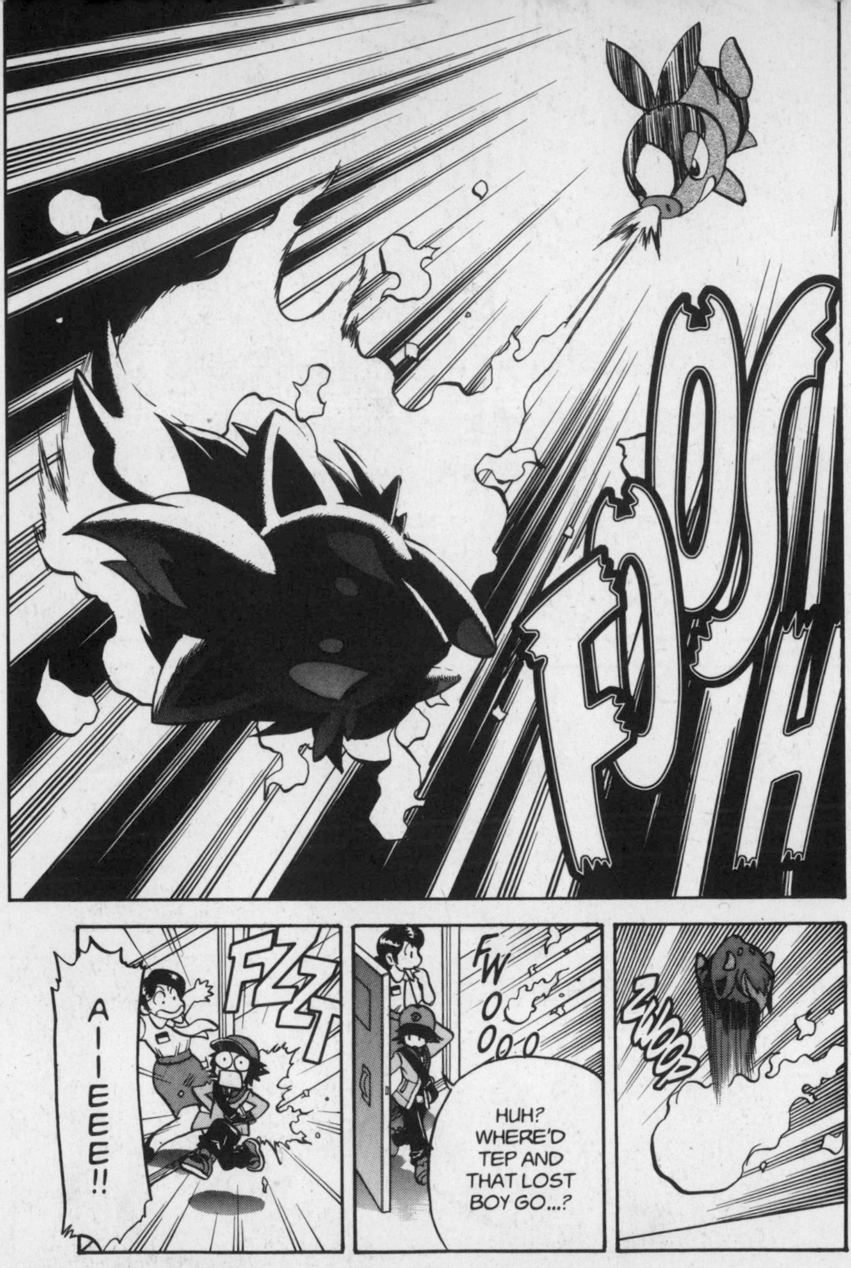
FOOSH
AIIEEE!!
FZZT
FWOOOOO
HUH? WHERE'D TEP AND THAT LOST BOY GO...?
ZWOOP

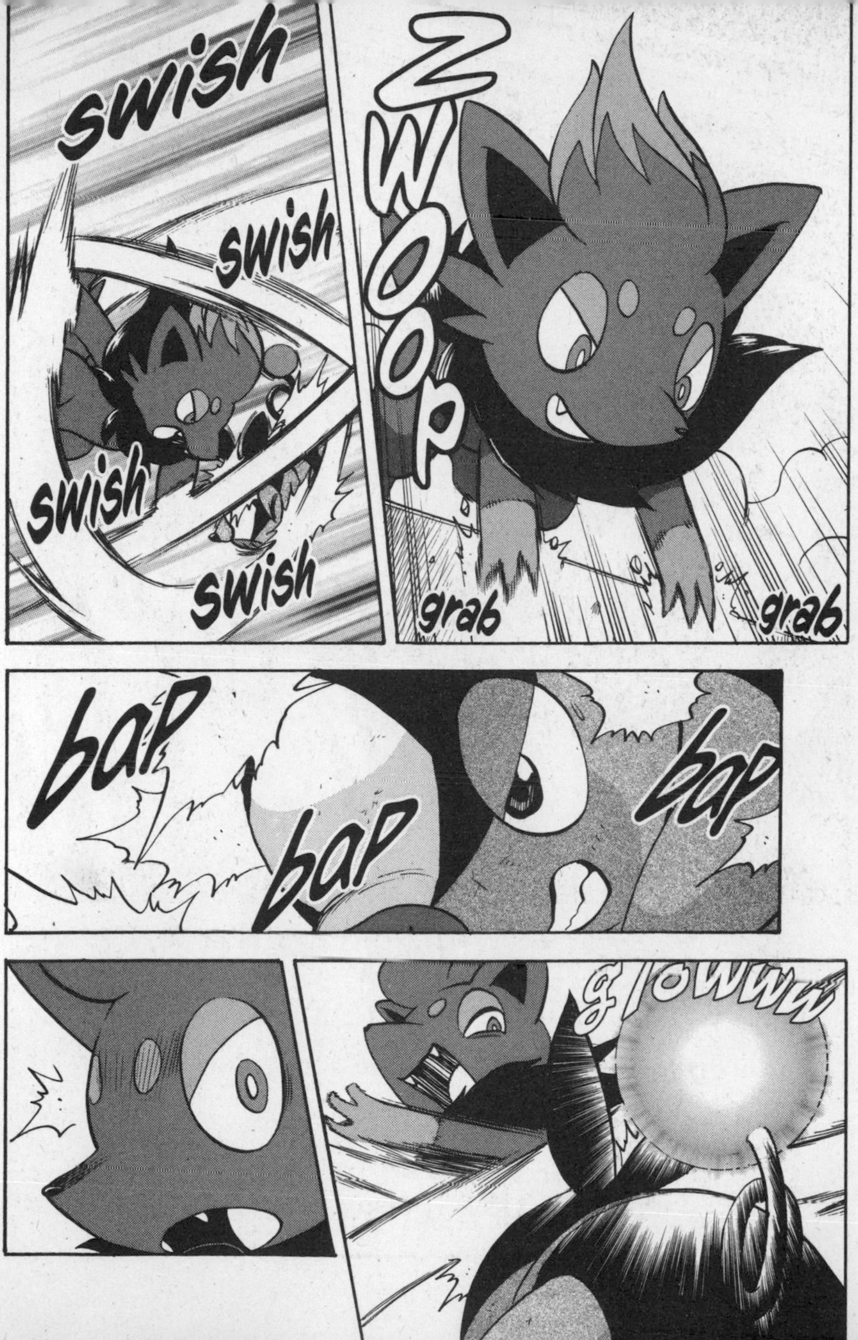
ZWOOOP
grab
grab
swish
swish
swish
swish
bap
bap
bap
glowww

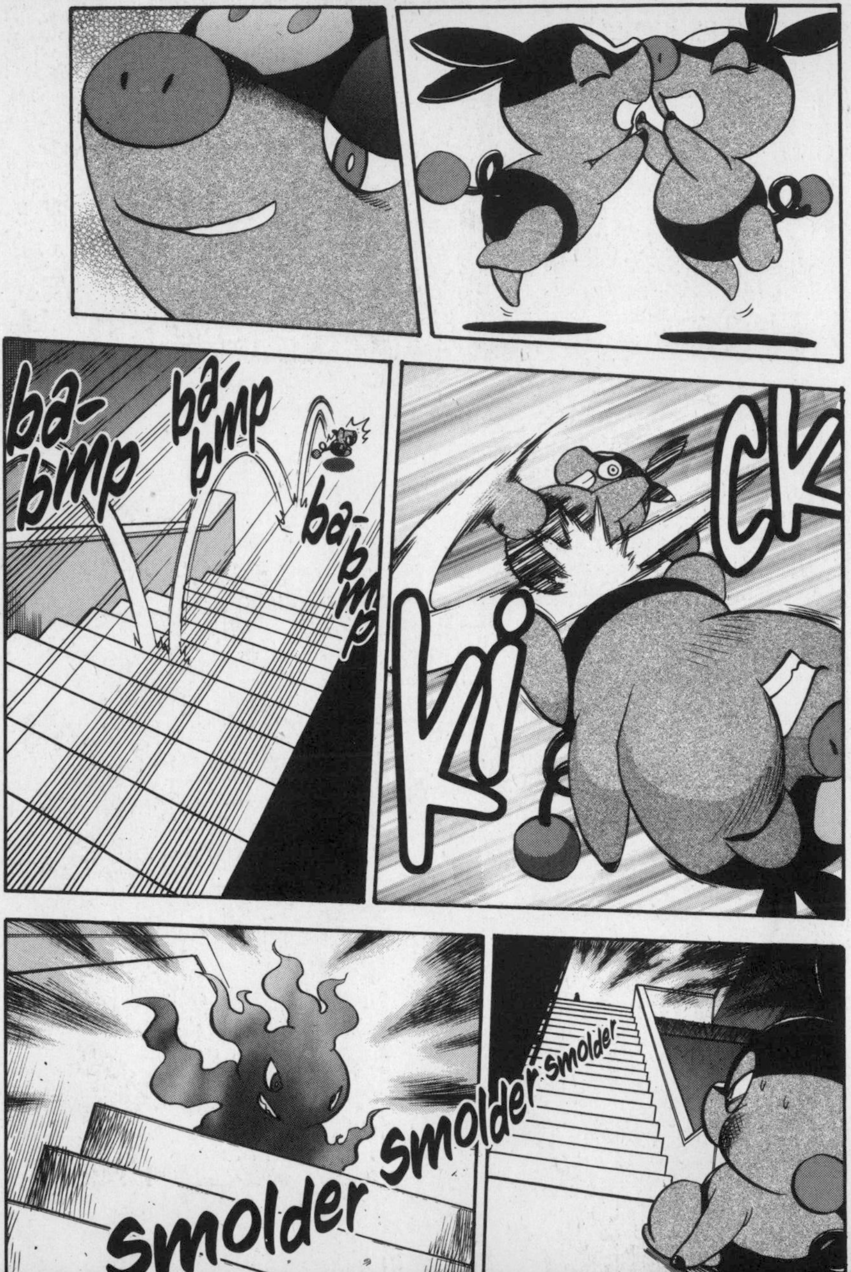

ba-bmp
ba-bmp
ba-bmp
kick
smolder
smolder
smolder

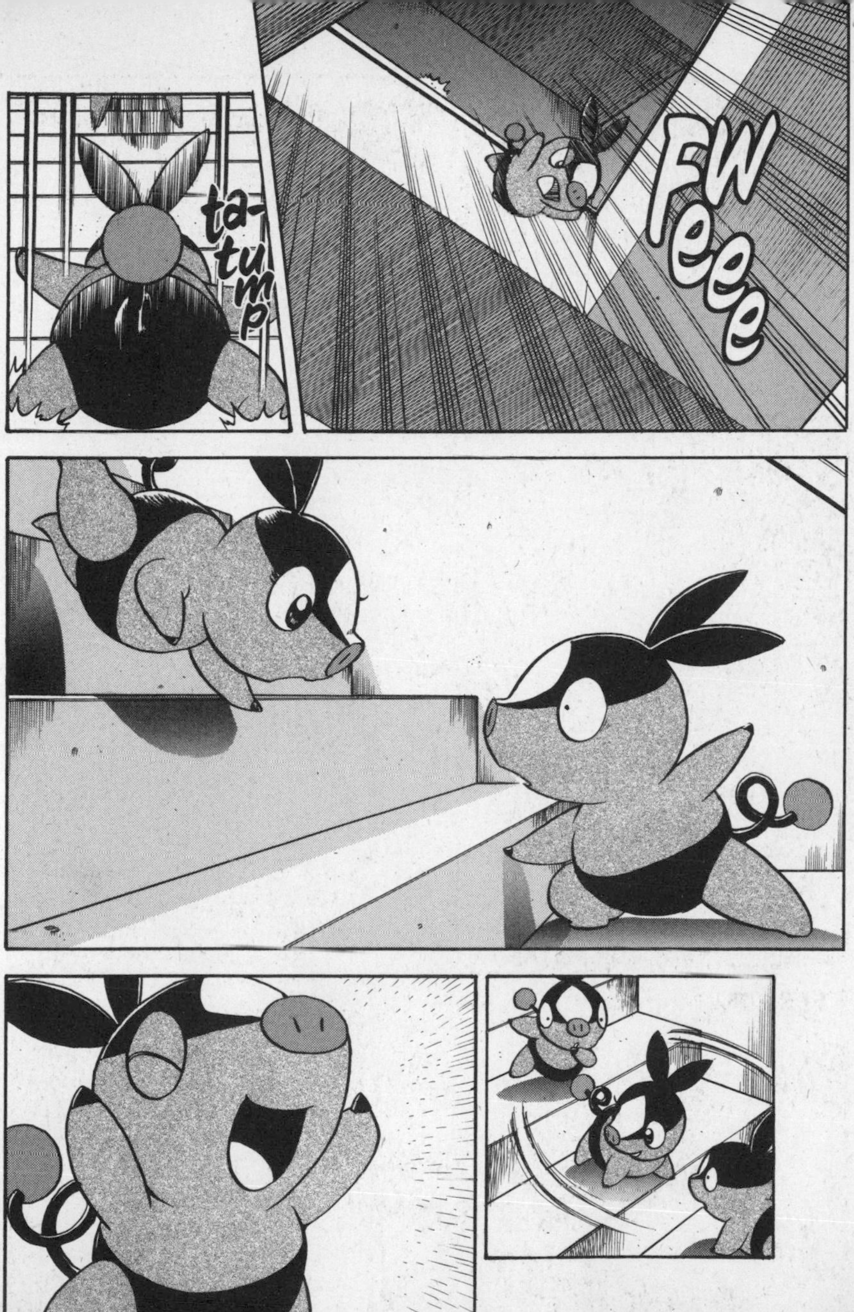
ta-
tump
FW
eeee

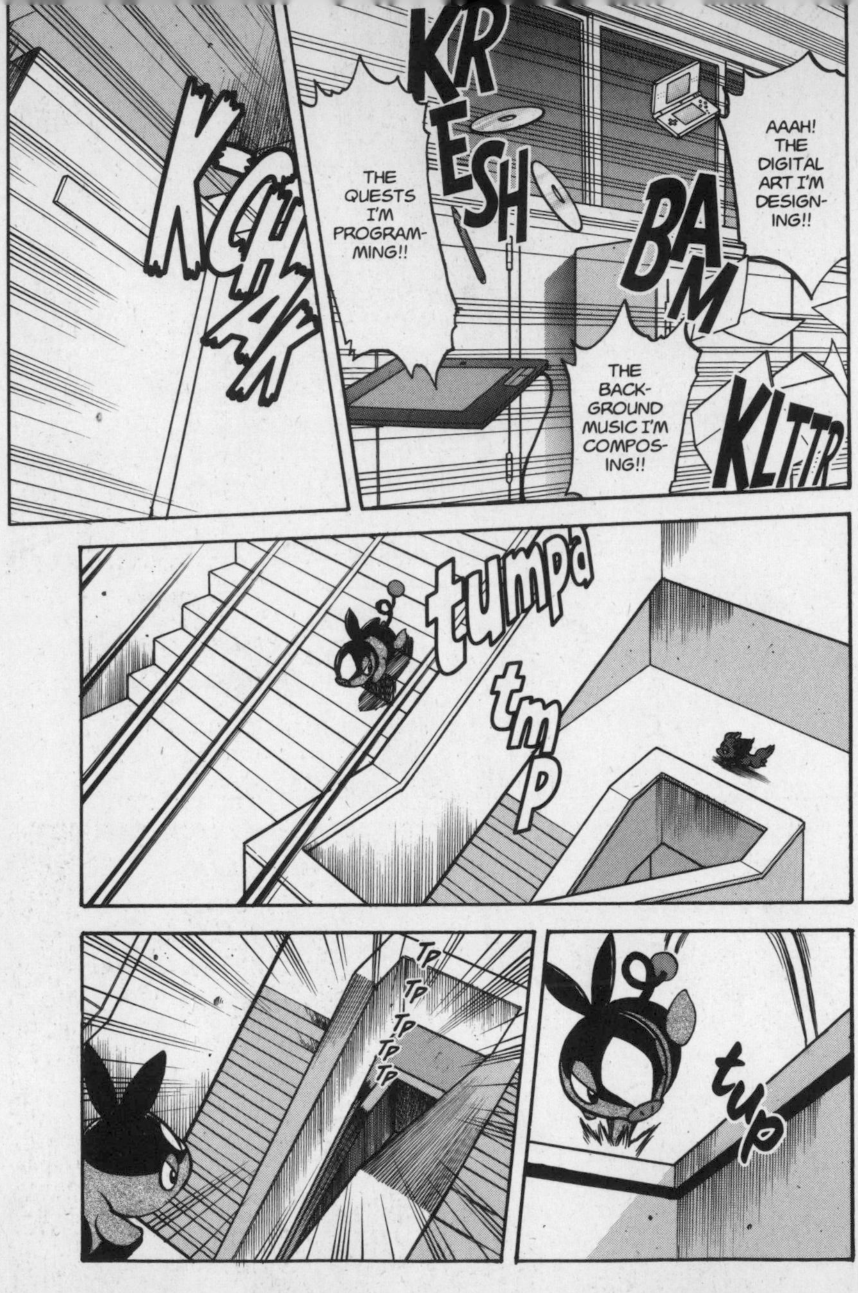
AAAH! THE DIGITAL ART I'M DESIGNING!!
THE QUESTS I'M PROGRAMMING!!
THE BACKGROUND MUSIC I'M COMPOSING!!
KR ESH
KCHAK
BAM
KLTTR
tumpa
tmp
TP TP TP TP TP
tup

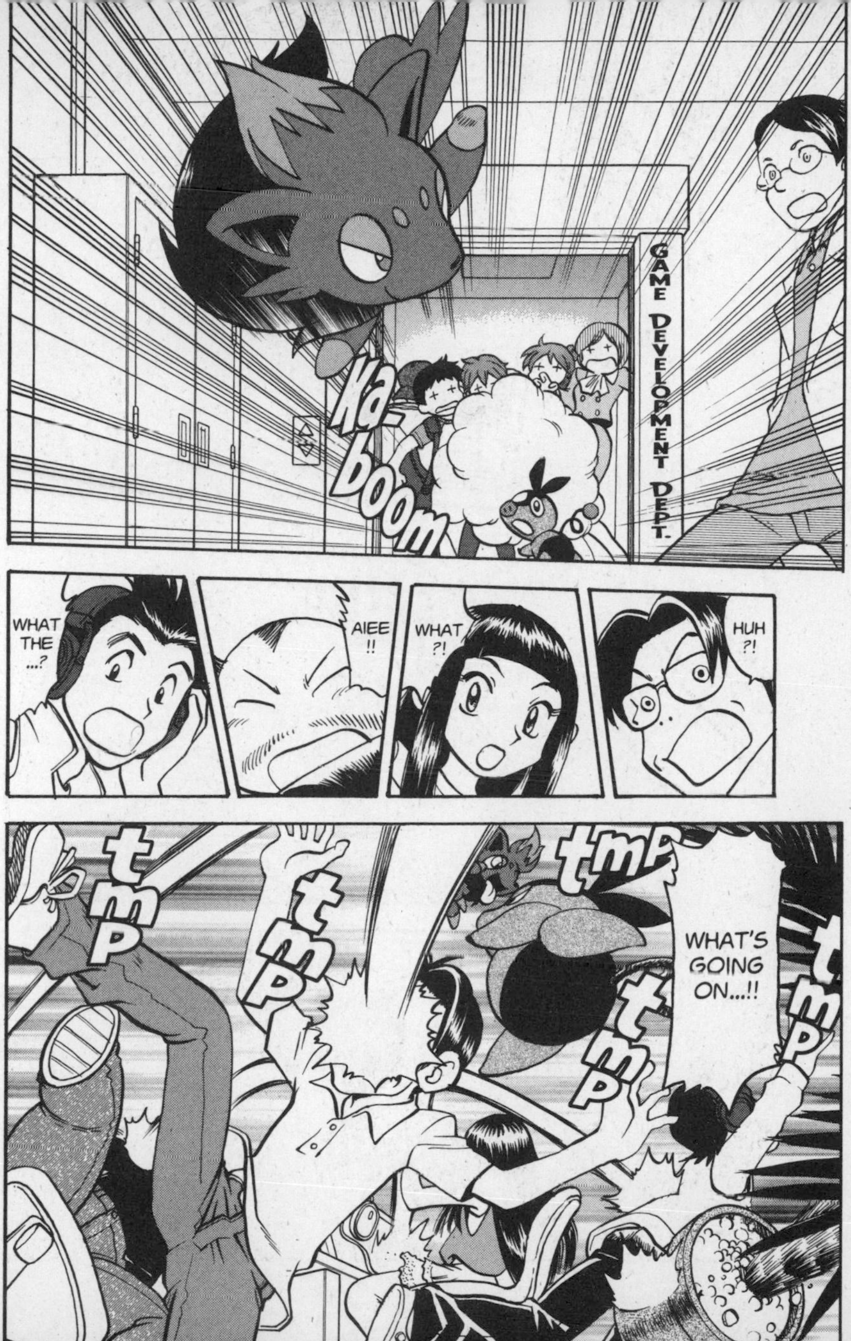
GAME DEVELOPMENT DEPT.
ka-boom
HUH ?!
WHAT ?!
AIEE !!
WHAT THE ...?
tmp
tmp
tmp
tmp
WHAT'S GOING ON...!!
tmp
tmp

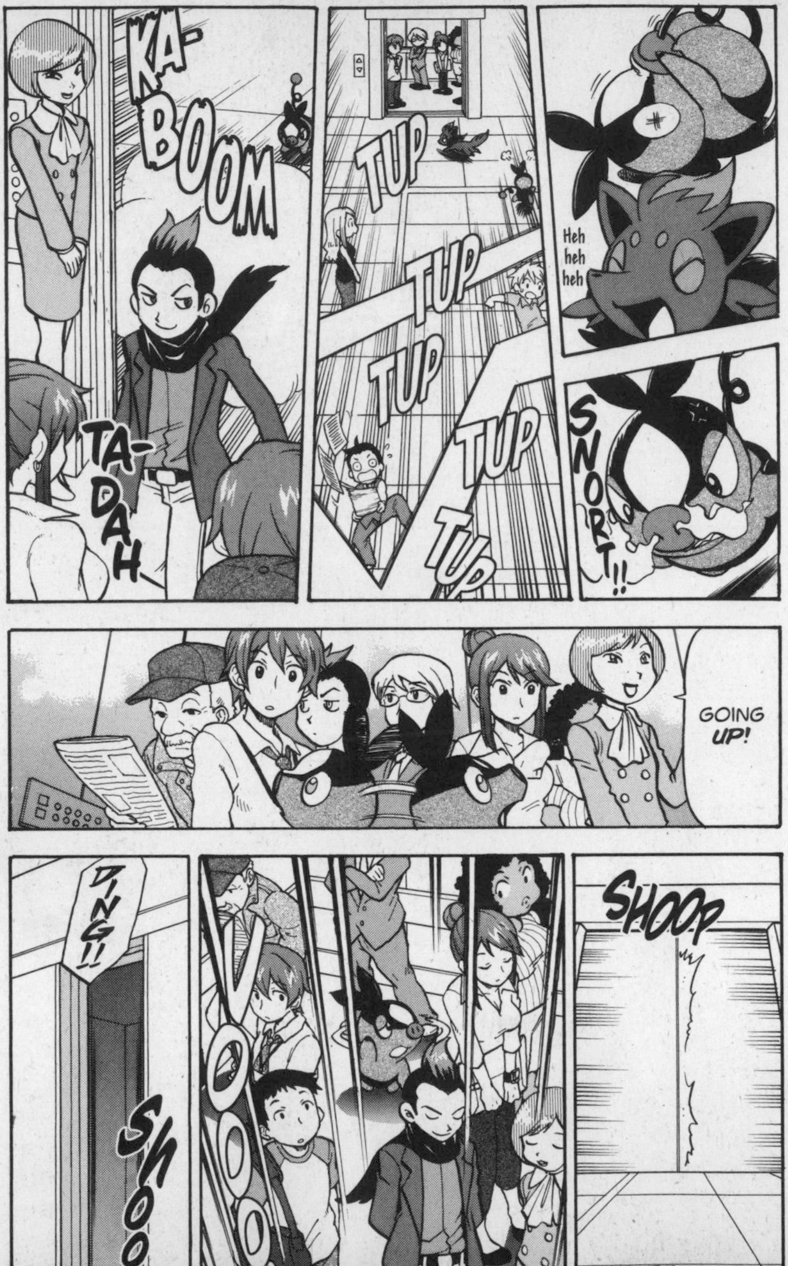
KA-BOOM
TA-DAH
TUP
TUP
TUP
TUP
TUP
Heh heh heh
SNORT!!
GOING UP!
DING!!
SHOOP
SHOO
VOOOOO

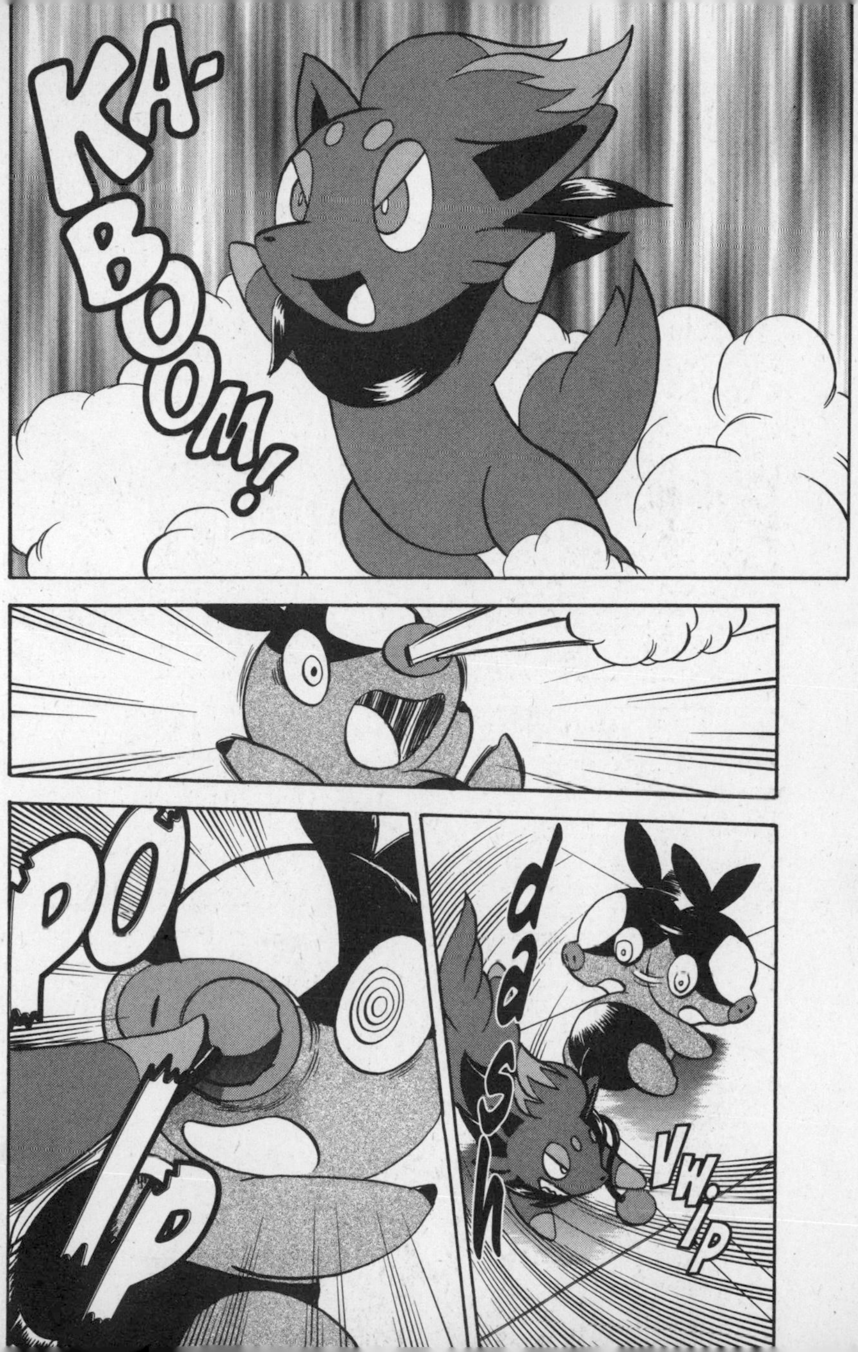
KA-BOOM!
POP
dash
WHIP
WHIP

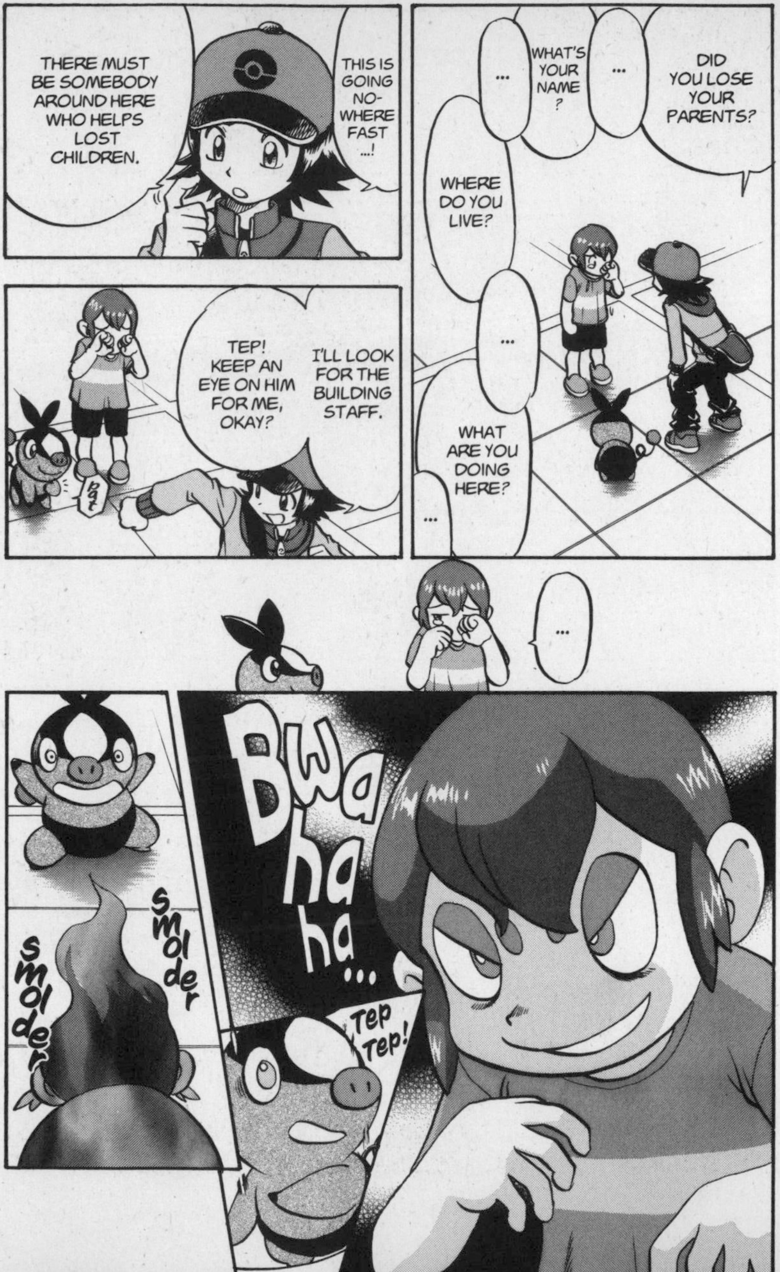
DID YOU LOSE YOUR PARENTS?
...
WHAT'S YOUR NAME?
...
WHERE DO YOU LIVE?
...
WHAT ARE YOU DOING HERE?
...
THIS IS GOING NO-WHERE FAST ...!
THERE MUST BE SOMEBODY AROUND HERE WHO HELPS LOST CHILDREN.
TEP! KEEP AN EYE ON HIM FOR ME, OKAY?
I'LL LOOK FOR THE BUILDING STAFF.
pat
...
Bwa ha ha...
smolder smolder
Tep Tep!

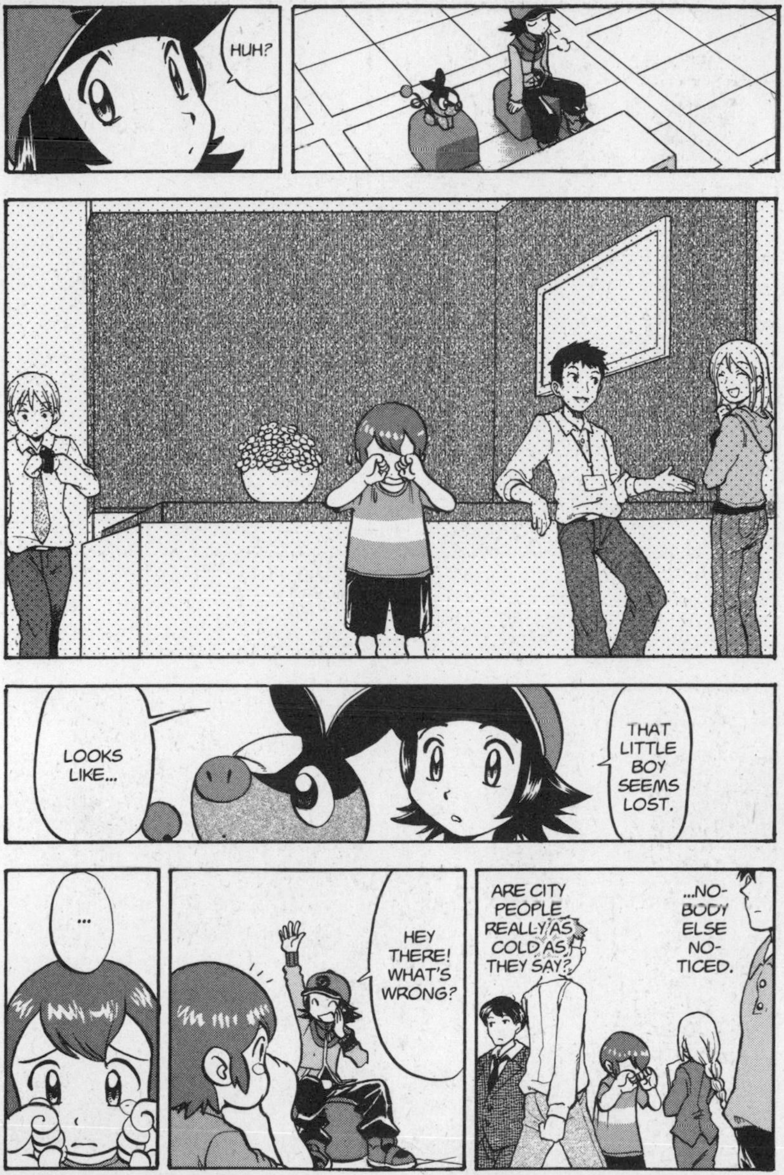
HUH?
LOOKS LIKE...
THAT LITTLE BOY SEEMS LOST.
...
HEY THERE! WHAT'S WRONG?
ARE CITY PEOPLE REALLY AS COLD AS THEY SAY?
...NO-BODY ELSE NO-TICED.

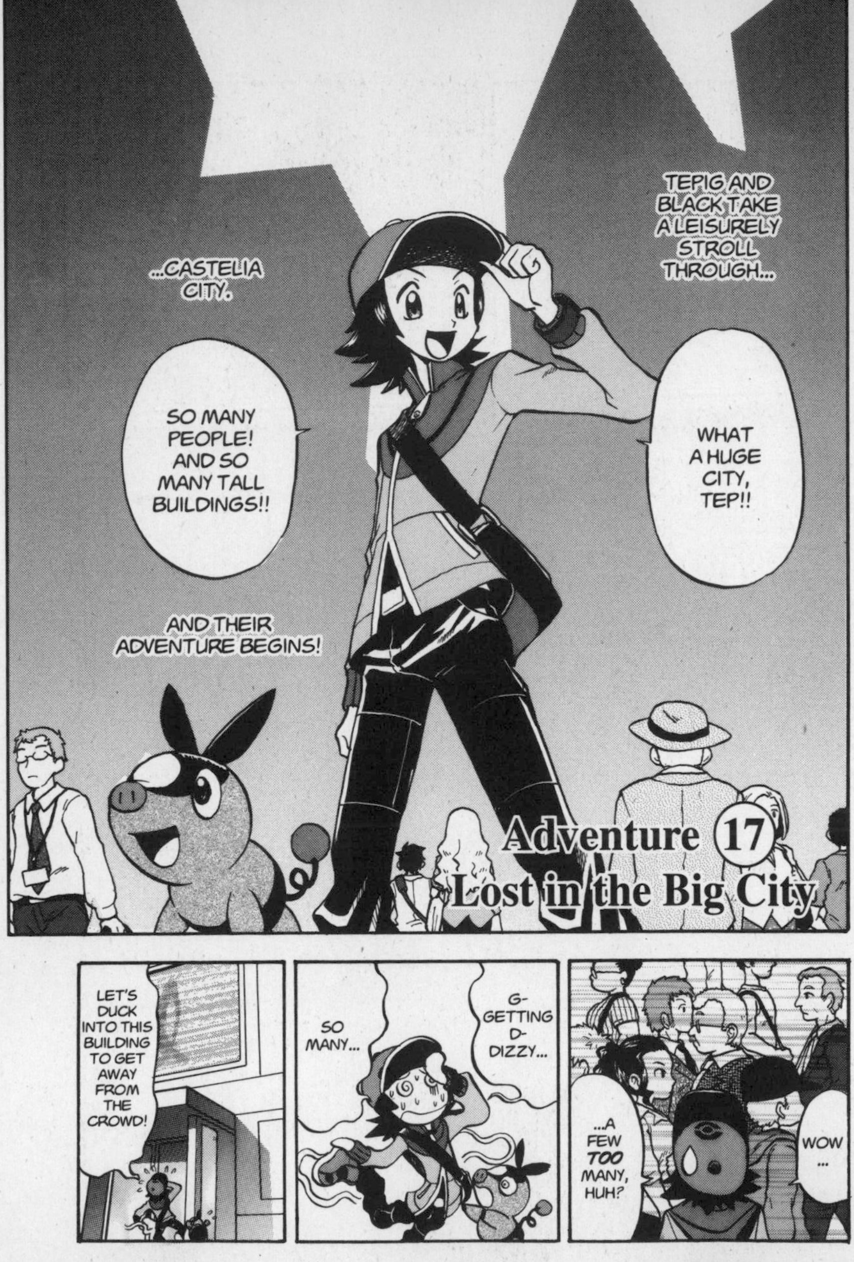
TEPIG AND BLACK TAKE A LEISURELY STROLL THROUGH...
...CASTELIA CITY.
WHAT A HUGE CITY, TEP!!
SO MANY PEOPLE! AND SO MANY TALL BUILDINGS!!
AND THEIR ADVENTURE BEGINS!
Adventure 17
Lost in the Big City
WOW...
...A FEW TOO MANY, HUH?
SO MANY...
G-GETTING D-DIZZY...
LET'S DUCK INTO THIS BUILDING TO GET AWAY FROM THE CROWD!

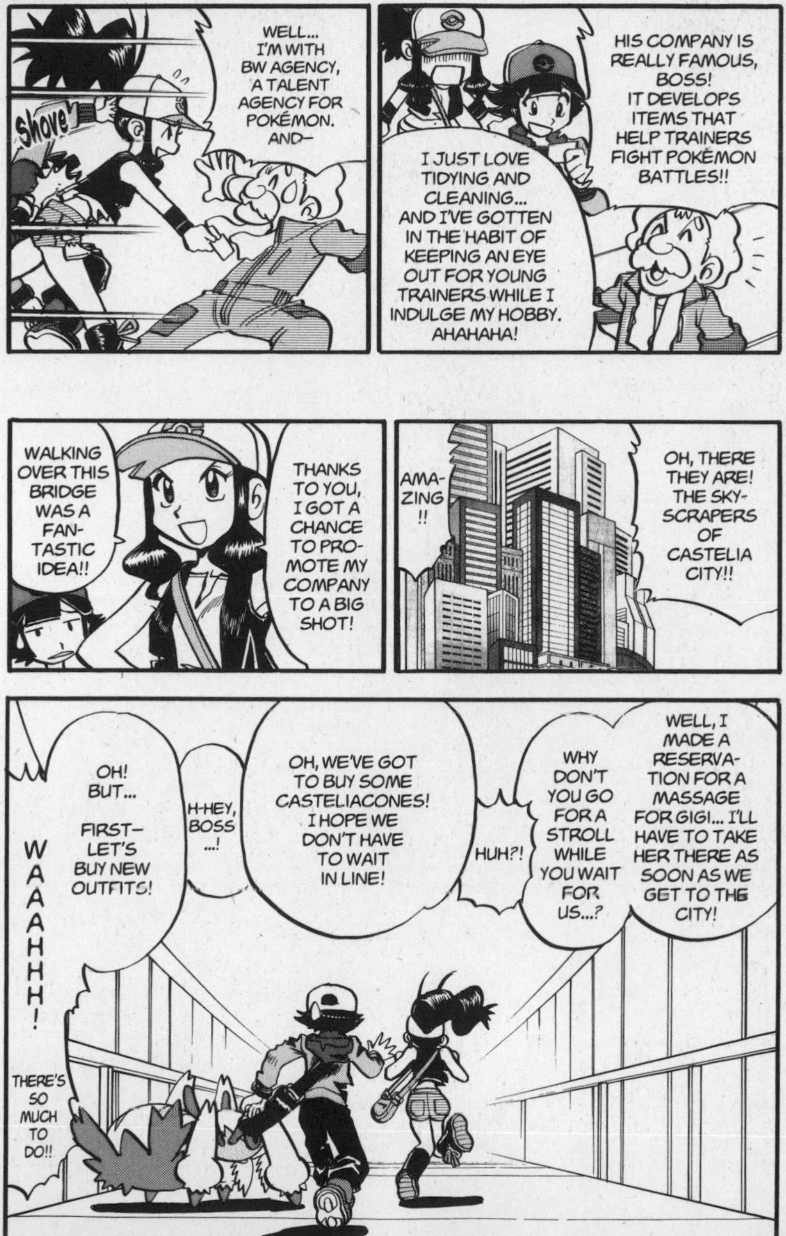
Shove
WELL... I'M WITH BW AGENCY, A TALENT AGENCY FOR POKÉMON. AND—
HIS COMPANY IS REALLY FAMOUS, BOSS! IT DEVELOPS ITEMS THAT HELP TRAINERS FIGHT POKÉMON BATTLES!!
I JUST LOVE TIDYING AND CLEANING... AND I'VE GOTTEN IN THE HABIT OF KEEPING AN EYE OUT FOR YOUNG TRAINERS WHILE I INDULGE MY HOBBY. AHAHAHA!
WALKING OVER THIS BRIDGE WAS A FANTASTIC IDEA!!
THANKS TO YOU, I GOT A CHANCE TO PROMOTE MY COMPANY TO A BIG SHOT!
OH, THERE THEY ARE! THE SKYSCRAPERS OF CASTELIA CITY!!
AMAZING!!
WELL, I MADE A RESERVATION FOR A MASSAGE FOR GIGI... I'LL HAVE TO TAKE HER THERE AS SOON AS WE GET TO THE CITY!
WHY DON'T YOU GO FOR A STROLL WHILE YOU WAIT FOR US...?
HUH?!
OH, WE'VE GOT TO BUY SOME CASTELIACONES! I HOPE WE DON'T HAVE TO WAIT IN LINE!
H-HEY, BOSS...!
OH! BUT... FIRST—LET'S BUY NEW OUTFITS!
WAAAHHH!
THERE'S SO MUCH TO DO!!

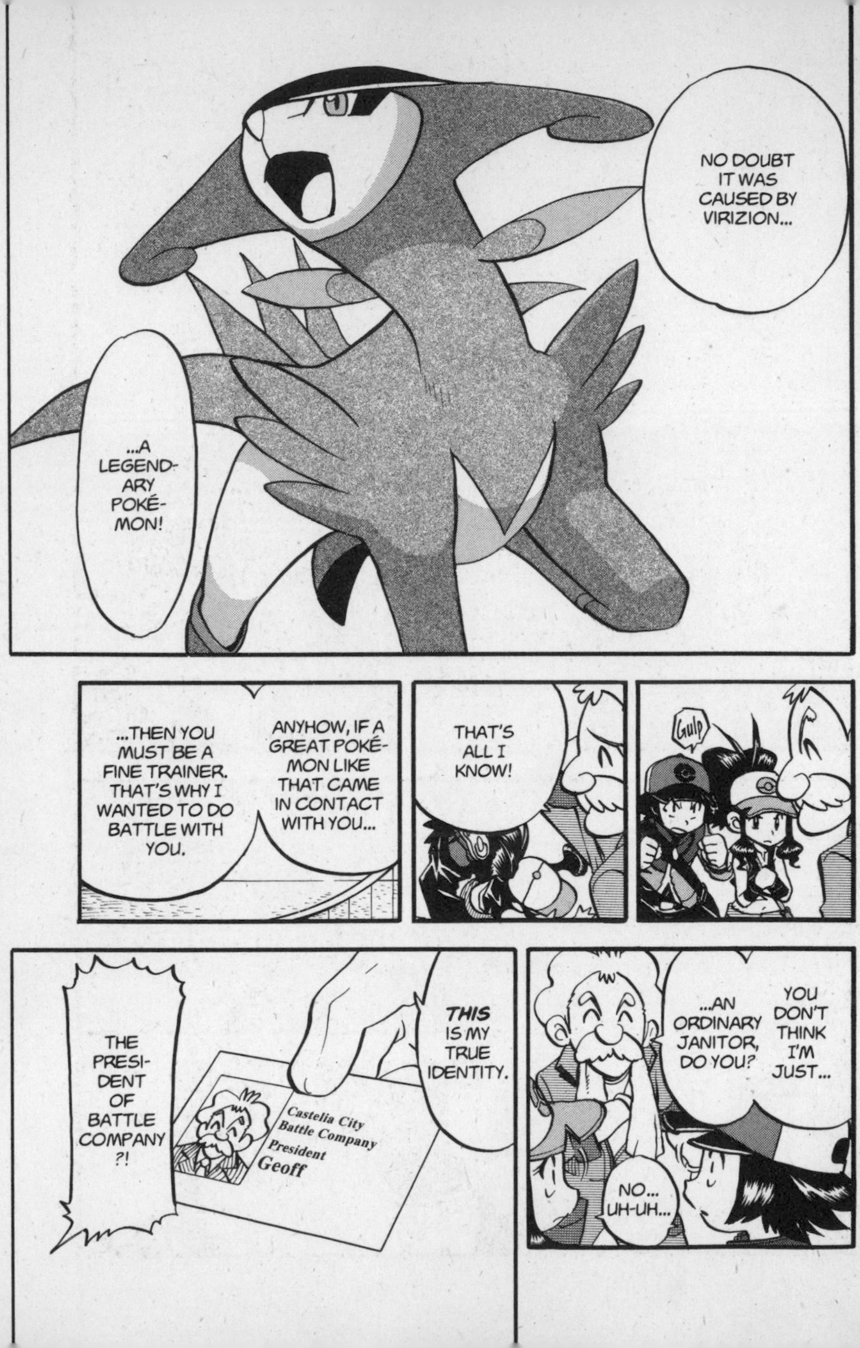
NO DOUBT IT WAS CAUSED BY VIRIZION...
...A LEGENDARY POKÉMON!
THAT'S ALL I KNOW!
ANYHOW, IF A GREAT POKÉMON LIKE THAT CAME IN CONTACT WITH YOU...
...THEN YOU MUST BE A FINE TRAINER. THAT'S WHY I WANTED TO DO BATTLE WITH YOU.
Gulp
YOU DON'T THINK I'M JUST...
...AN ORDINARY JANITOR, DO YOU?
NO... UH-UH...
THIS IS MY TRUE IDENTITY.
Castelia City Battle Company President Geoff
THE PRESIDENT OF BATTLE COMPANY?!

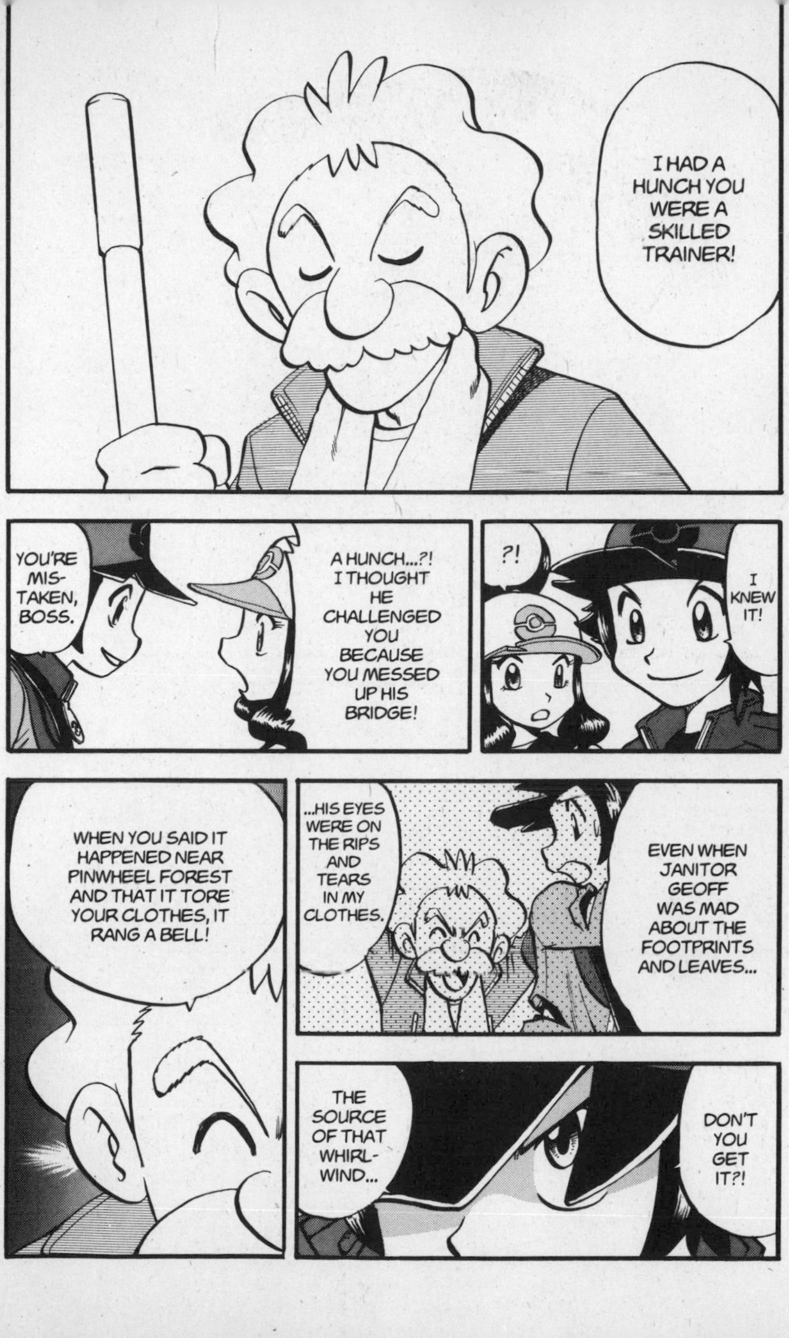
I HAD A HUNCH YOU WERE A SKILLED TRAINER!
YOU'RE MIS-TAKEN, BOSS.
A HUNCH...?! I THOUGHT HE CHALLENGED YOU BECAUSE YOU MESSED UP HIS BRIDGE!
?!
I KNEW IT!
WHEN YOU SAID IT HAPPENED NEAR PINWHEEL FOREST AND THAT IT TORE YOUR CLOTHES, IT RANG A BELL!
...HIS EYES WERE ON THE RIPS AND TEARS IN MY CLOTHES.
EVEN WHEN JANITOR GEOFF WAS MAD ABOUT THE FOOTPRINTS AND LEAVES...
THE SOURCE OF THAT WHIRL-WIND...
DON'T YOU GET IT?!

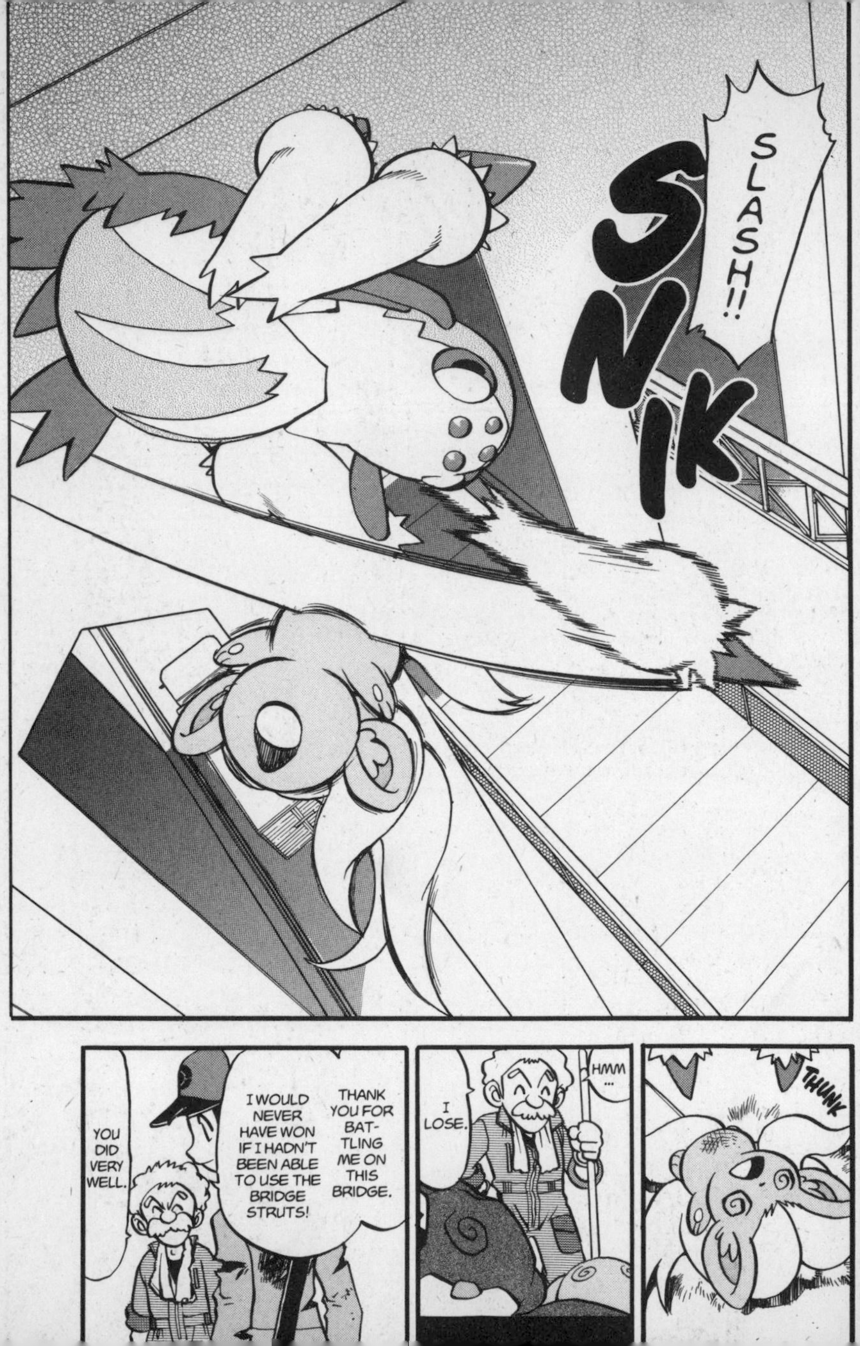
SNIK
SLASH!!
THUNK
HMM...
I LOSE.
YOU DID VERY WELL.
I WOULD NEVER HAVE WON IF I HADN'T BEEN ABLE TO USE THE BRIDGE STRUTS!
THANK YOU FOR BATTLING ME ON THIS BRIDGE.

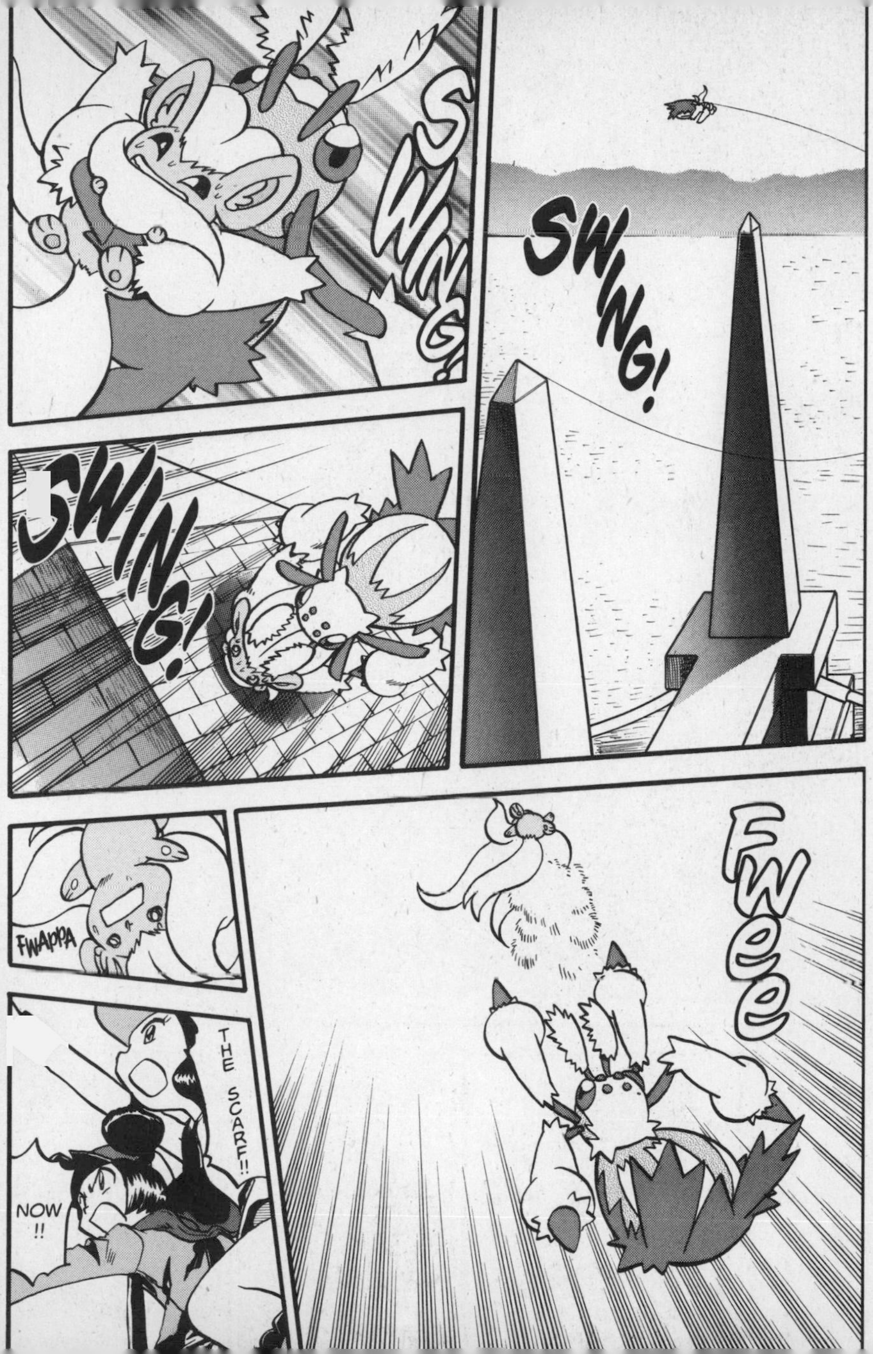
SWING!
SWING!
SWING!
FWAPPA
Fwee
THE SCARF!!
NOW!!

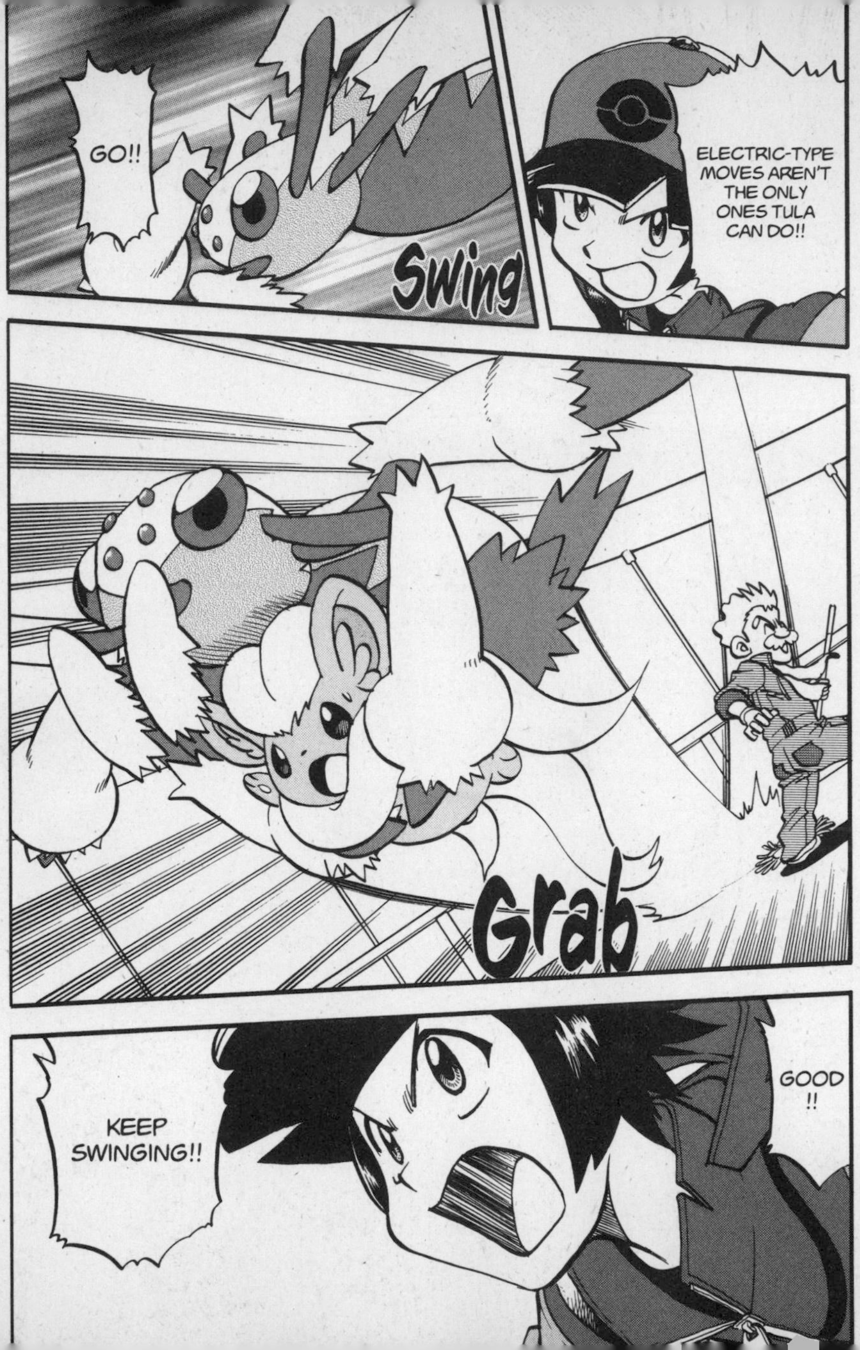
GO!!
ELECTRIC-TYPE MOVES AREN'T THE ONLY ONES TULA CAN DO!!
Swing
Grab
GOOD !!
KEEP SWINGING!!

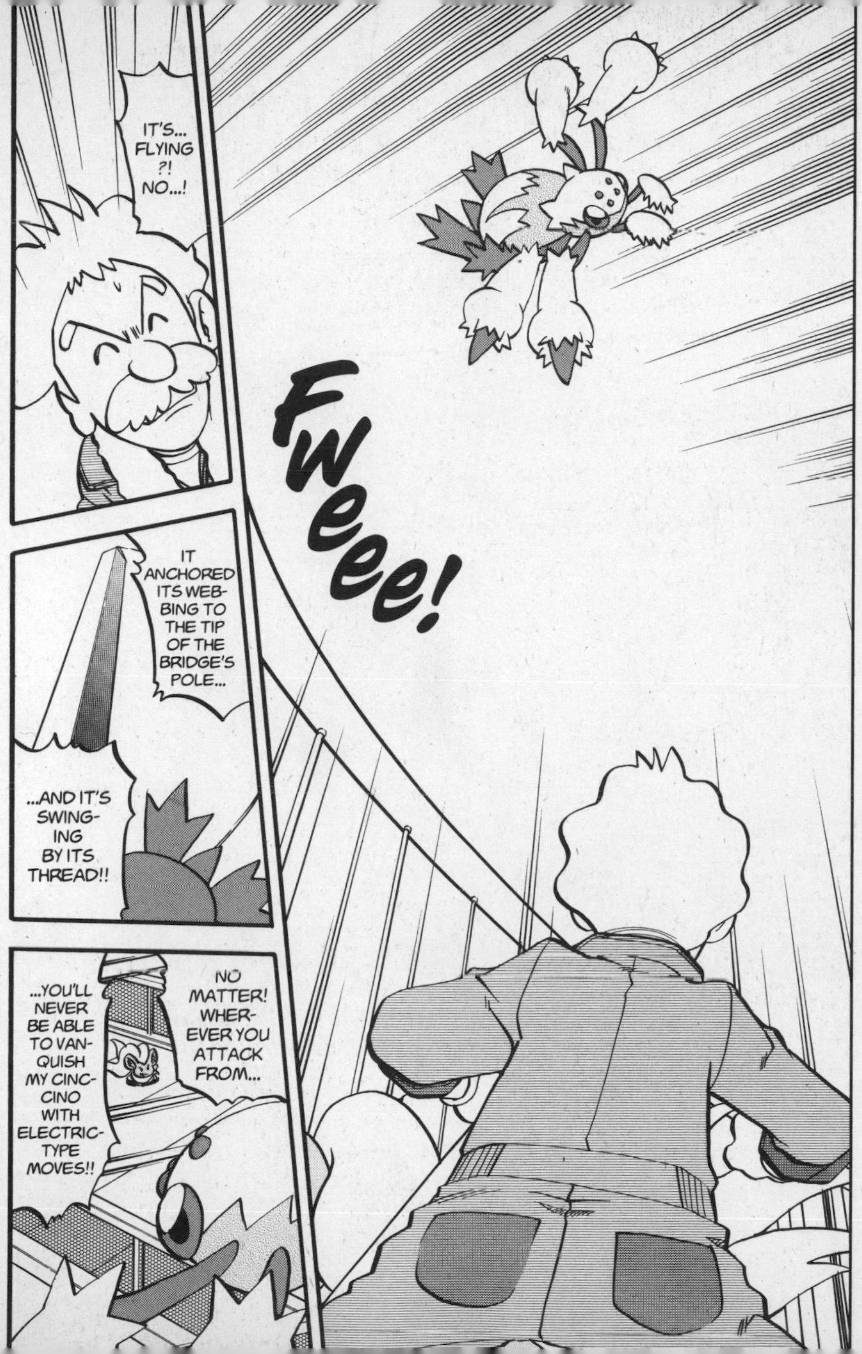
IT'S... FLYING?! NO...!
Fweee!
IT ANCHORED ITS WEB-BING TO THE TIP OF THE BRIDGE'S POLE...
...AND IT'S SWING-ING BY ITS THREAD!!
NO MATTER! WHER-EVER YOU ATTACK FROM...
...YOU'LL NEVER BE ABLE TO VAN-QUISH MY CINC-CINO WITH ELECTRIC-TYPE MOVES!!

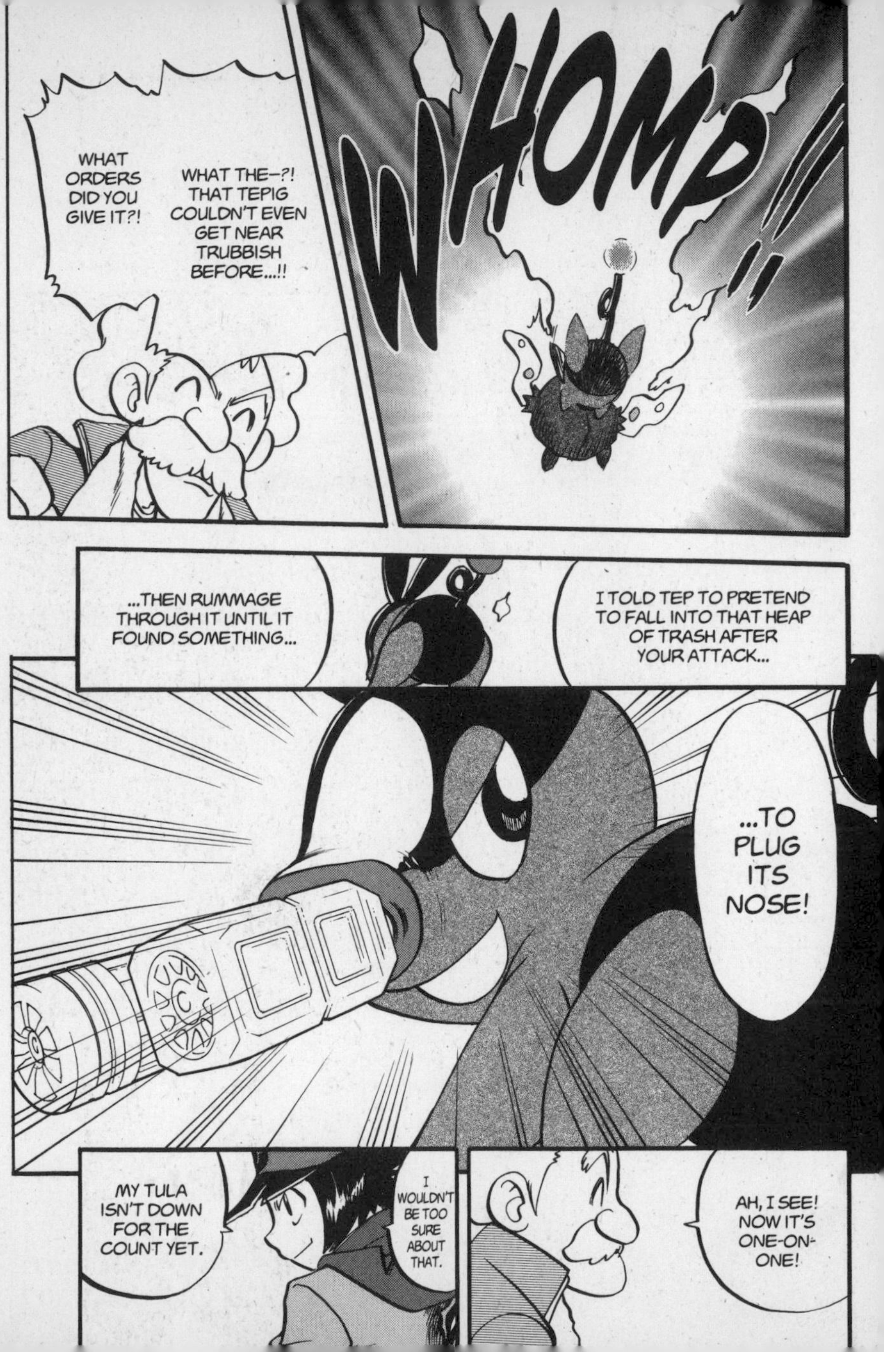
WHOMP!!
WHAT THE–?! THAT TEPIG COULDN'T EVEN GET NEAR TRUBBISH BEFORE...!!
WHAT ORDERS DID YOU GIVE IT?!
I TOLD TEP TO PRETEND TO FALL INTO THAT HEAP OF TRASH AFTER YOUR ATTACK...
...THEN RUMMAGE THROUGH IT UNTIL IT FOUND SOMETHING...
...TO PLUG ITS NOSE!
AH, I SEE! NOW IT'S ONE-ON-ONE!
I WOULDN'T BE TOO SURE ABOUT THAT.
MY TULA ISN'T DOWN FOR THE COUNT YET.

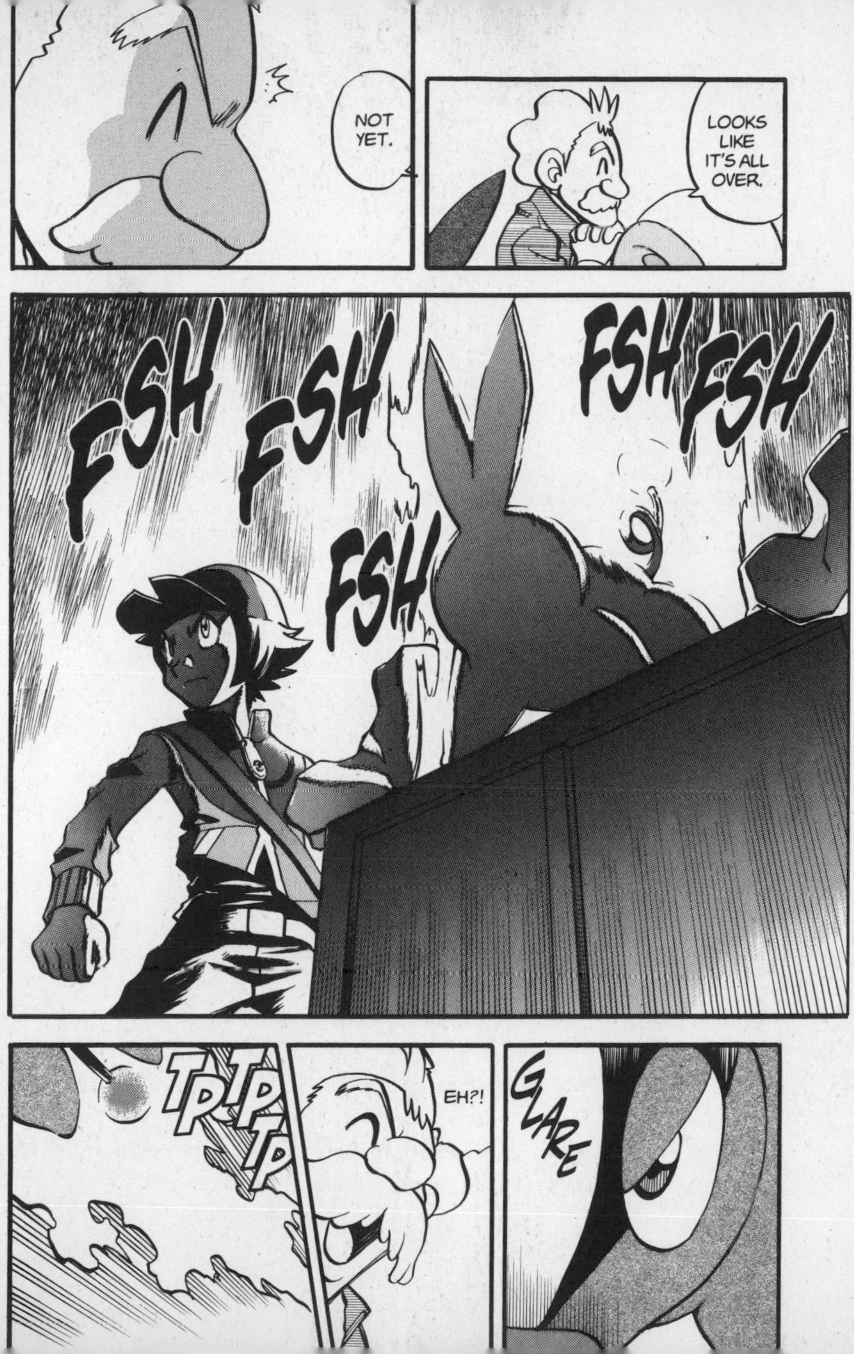
NOT YET.
LOOKS LIKE IT'S ALL OVER.
FSH FSH FSH FSH FSH
TP TP TP TP
EH?!
GLARE

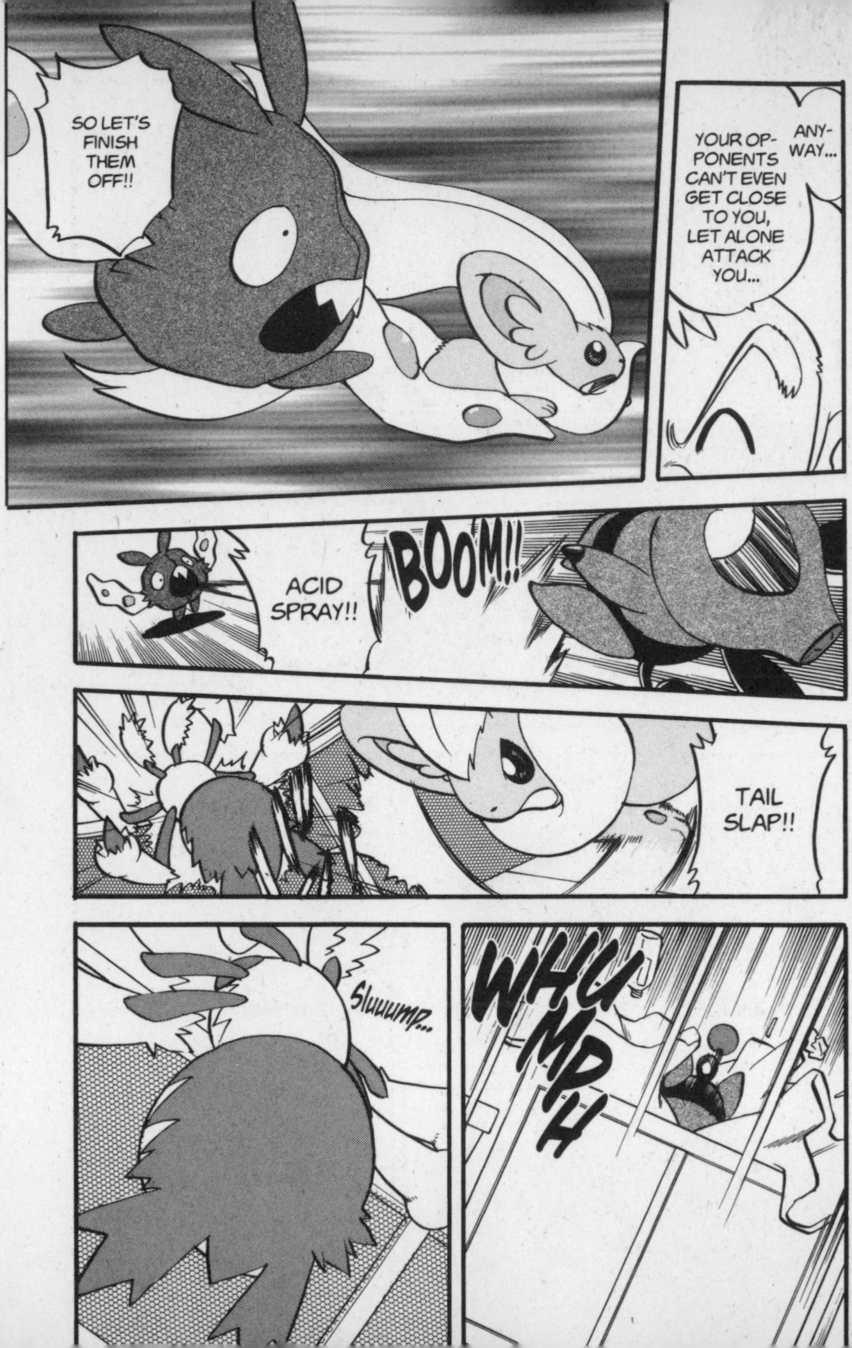
ANY-WAY...
YOUR OP-PONENTS CAN'T EVEN GET CLOSE TO YOU, LET ALONE ATTACK YOU...
SO LET'S FINISH THEM OFF!!
BOOM!!
ACID SPRAY!!
TAIL SLAP!!
WHUMPH
Sluuump...

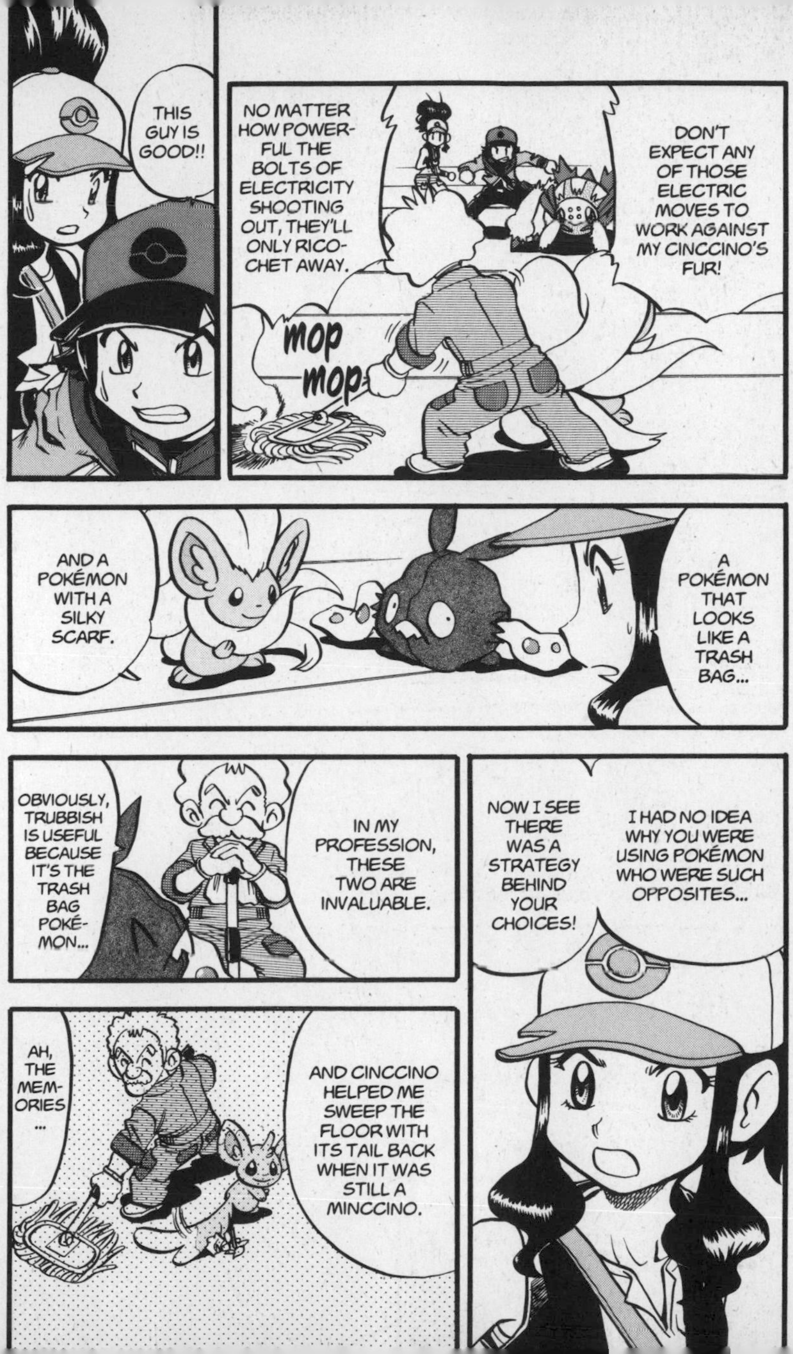
THIS GUY IS GOOD!!
NO MATTER HOW POWERFUL THE BOLTS OF ELECTRICITY SHOOTING OUT, THEY'LL ONLY RICOCHET AWAY.
DON'T EXPECT ANY OF THOSE ELECTRIC MOVES TO WORK AGAINST MY CINCCINO'S FUR!
mop mop
A POKÉMON THAT LOOKS LIKE A TRASH BAG...
AND A POKÉMON WITH A SILKY SCARF.
I HAD NO IDEA WHY YOU WERE USING POKÉMON WHO WERE SUCH OPPOSITES...
NOW I SEE THERE WAS A STRATEGY BEHIND YOUR CHOICES!
IN MY PROFESSION, THESE TWO ARE INVALUABLE.
OBVIOUSLY, TRUBBISH IS USEFUL BECAUSE IT'S THE TRASH BAG POKÉMON...
AND CINCCINO HELPED ME SWEEP THE FLOOR WITH ITS TAIL BACK WHEN IT WAS STILL A MINCCINO.
AH, THE MEMORIES...

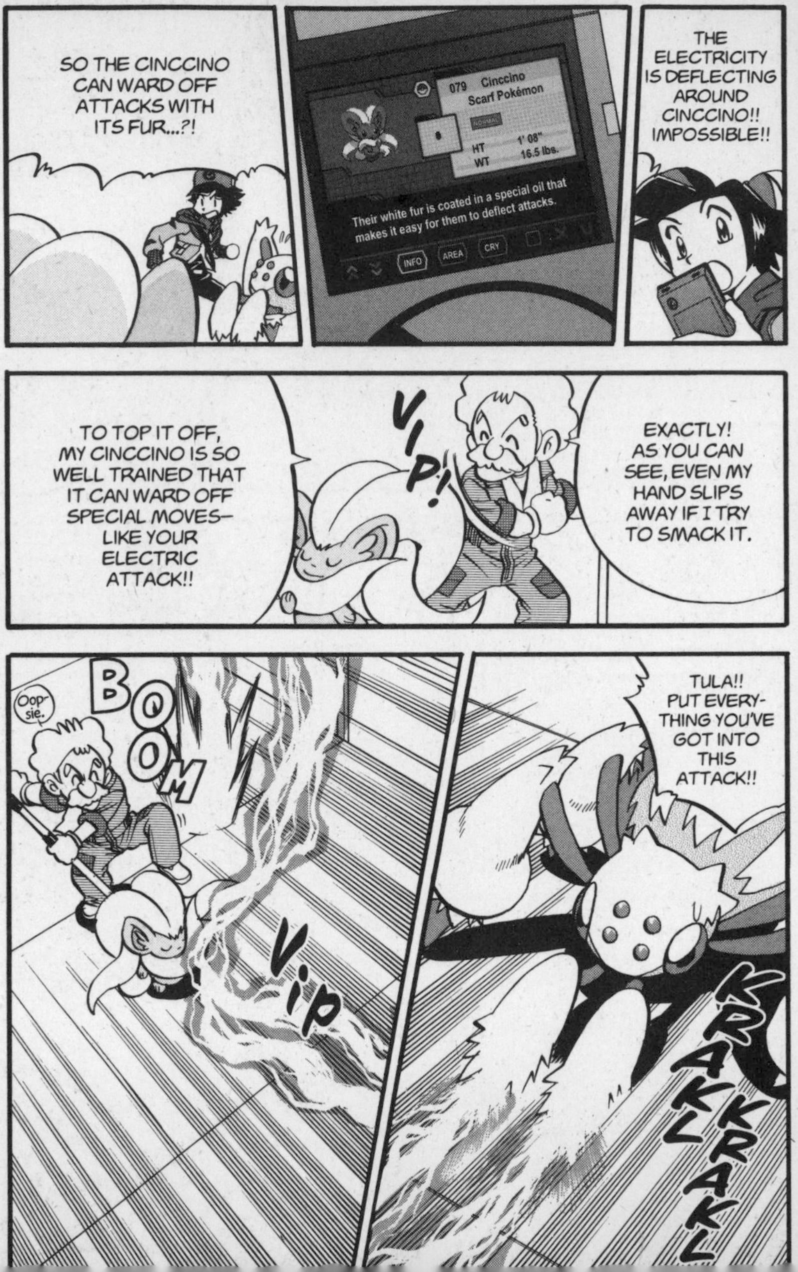
SO THE CINCCINO CAN WARD OFF ATTACKS WITH ITS FUR...?!
079 Cinccino
Scarf Pokémon
HT 1' 08"
WT 16.5 lbs.
Their white fur is coated in a special oil that makes it easy for them to deflect attacks.
INFO
AREA
CRY
THE ELECTRICITY IS DEFLECTING AROUND CINCCINO!! IMPOSSIBLE!!
TO TOP IT OFF, MY CINCCINO IS SO WELL TRAINED THAT IT CAN WARD OFF SPECIAL MOVES—LIKE YOUR ELECTRIC ATTACK!!
VIP!
EXACTLY! AS YOU CAN SEE, EVEN MY HAND SLIPS AWAY IF I TRY TO SMACK IT.
Oop-sie.
BOOOM
Vip
TULA!! PUT EVERY-THING YOU'VE GOT INTO THIS ATTACK!!
KRAKL KRAKL KRAKL

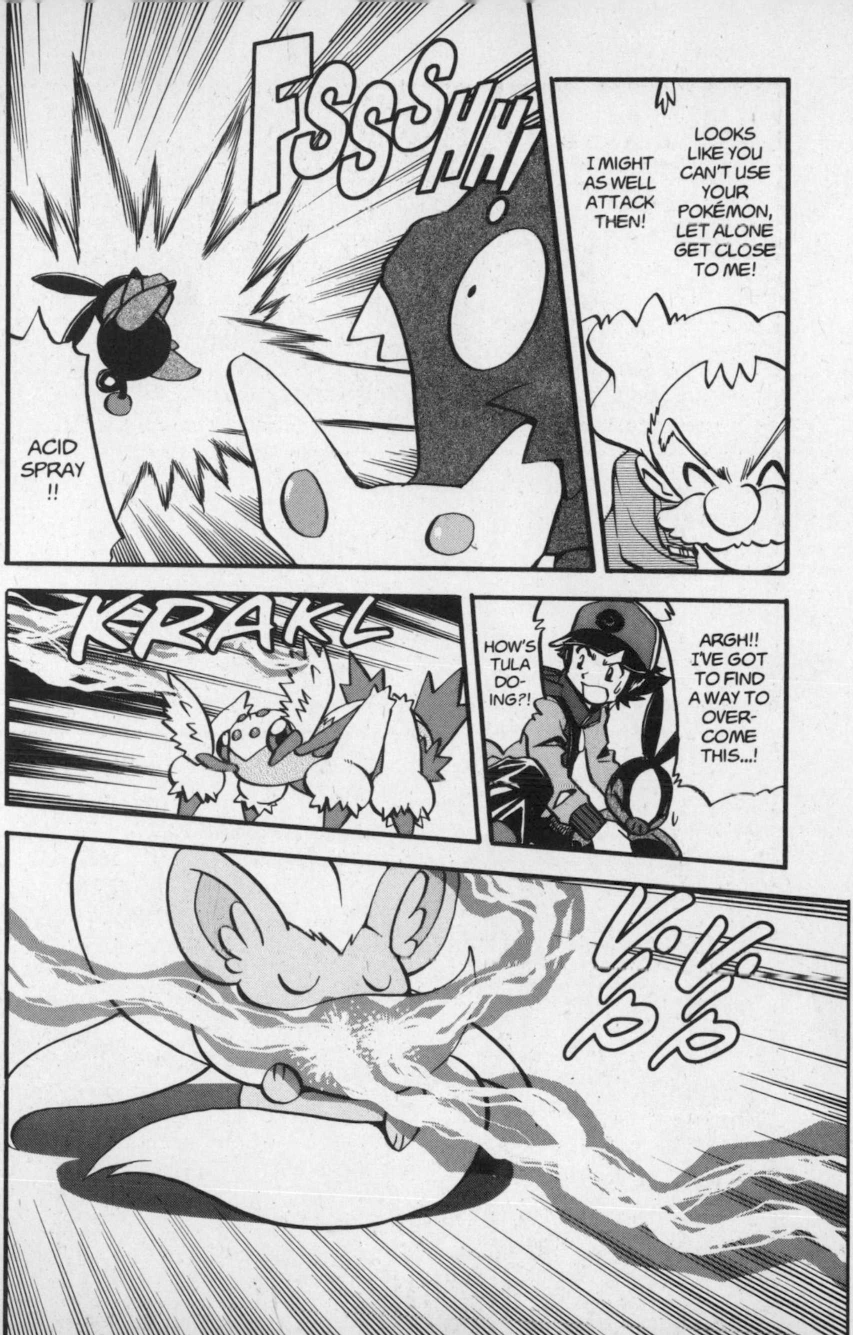
FSSSHH!
ACID SPRAY !!
LOOKS LIKE YOU CAN'T USE YOUR POKÉMON, LET ALONE GET CLOSE TO ME!
I MIGHT AS WELL ATTACK THEN!
KRAKL
HOW'S TULA DO-ING?!
ARGH!! I'VE GOT TO FIND A WAY TO OVER-COME THIS...!
V-V-VPPP

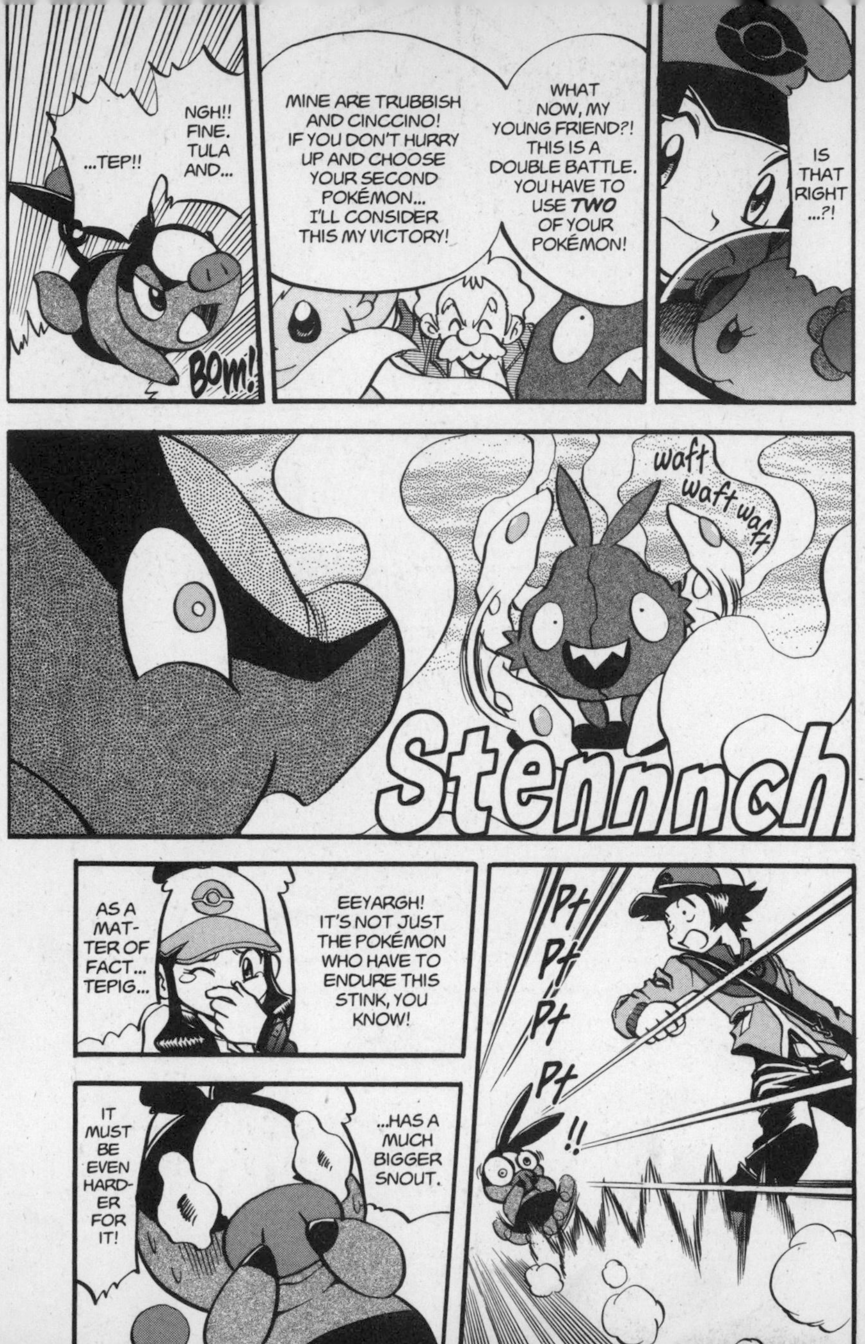

NGH!! FINE. TULA AND...
...TEP!!
BOM!
MINE ARE TRUBBISH AND CINCCINO! IF YOU DON'T HURRY UP AND CHOOSE YOUR SECOND POKÉMON... I'LL CONSIDER THIS MY VICTORY!
WHAT NOW, MY YOUNG FRIEND?! THIS IS A DOUBLE BATTLE. YOU HAVE TO USE TWO OF YOUR POKÉMON!
IS THAT RIGHT ...?!
waft waft waft waft
Stennnch
AS A MAT-TER OF FACT... TEPIG...
EEYARGH! IT'S NOT JUST THE POKÉMON WHO HAVE TO ENDURE THIS STINK, YOU KNOW!
Pt Pt Pt Pt
!!
IT MUST BE EVEN HARD-ER FOR IT!
...HAS A MUCH BIGGER SNOUT.

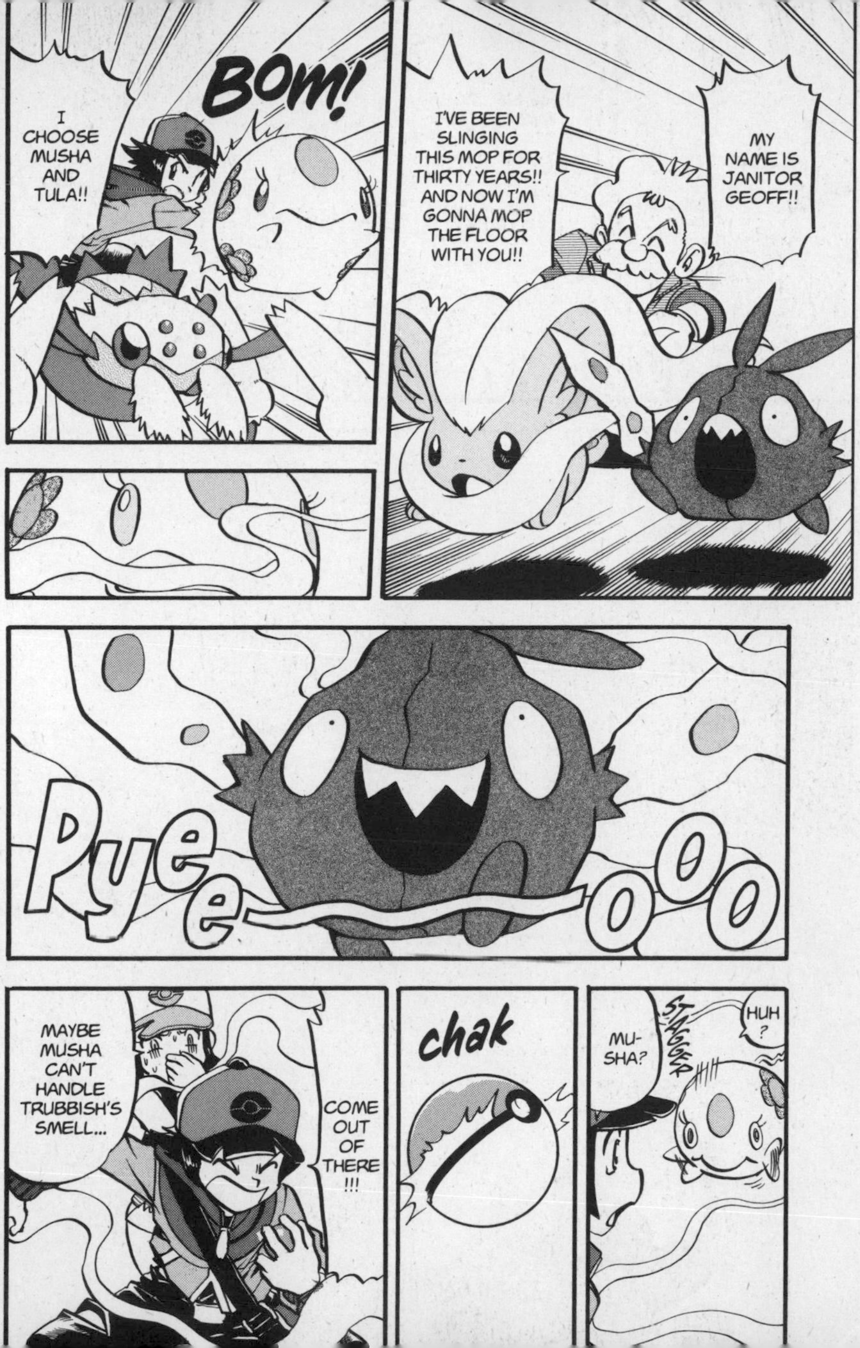
BOM!
I CHOOSE MUSHA AND TULA!!
I'VE BEEN SLINGING THIS MOP FOR THIRTY YEARS!! AND NOW I'M GONNA MOP THE FLOOR WITH YOU!!
MY NAME IS JANITOR GEOFF!!
Pyee-ooo
MAYBE MUSHA CAN'T HANDLE TRUBBISH'S SMELL...
COME OUT OF THERE!!!
chak
MU-SHA?
STAGGER
HUH?

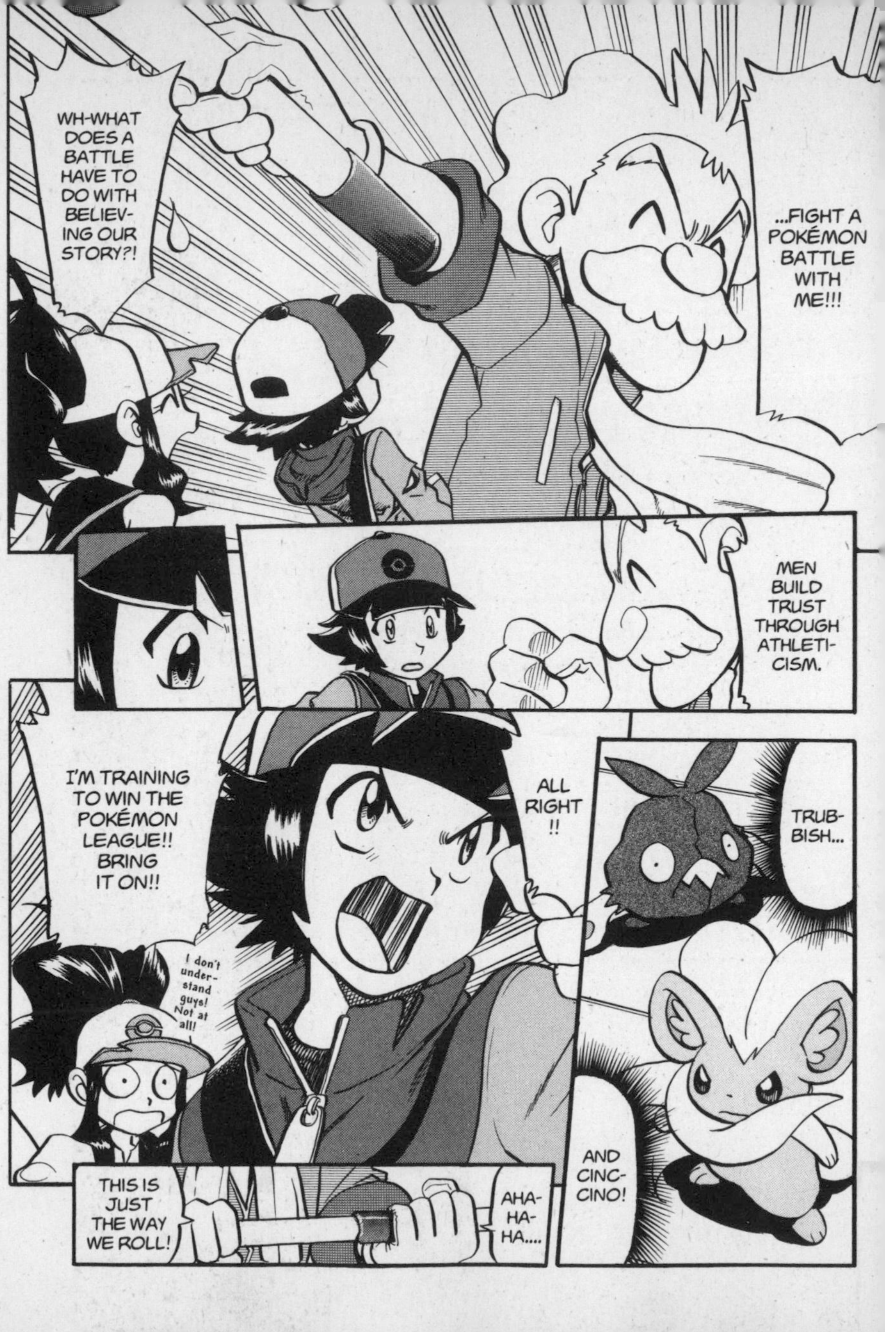
...FIGHT A POKÉMON BATTLE WITH ME!!!
WH-WHAT DOES A BATTLE HAVE TO DO WITH BELIEVING OUR STORY?!
MEN BUILD TRUST THROUGH ATHLETICISM.
ALL RIGHT!!
I'M TRAINING TO WIN THE POKÉMON LEAGUE!! BRING IT ON!!
TRUBBISH...
AND CINCCINO!
I don't understand guys! Not at all!
AHAHAHA....
THIS IS JUST THE WAY WE ROLL!

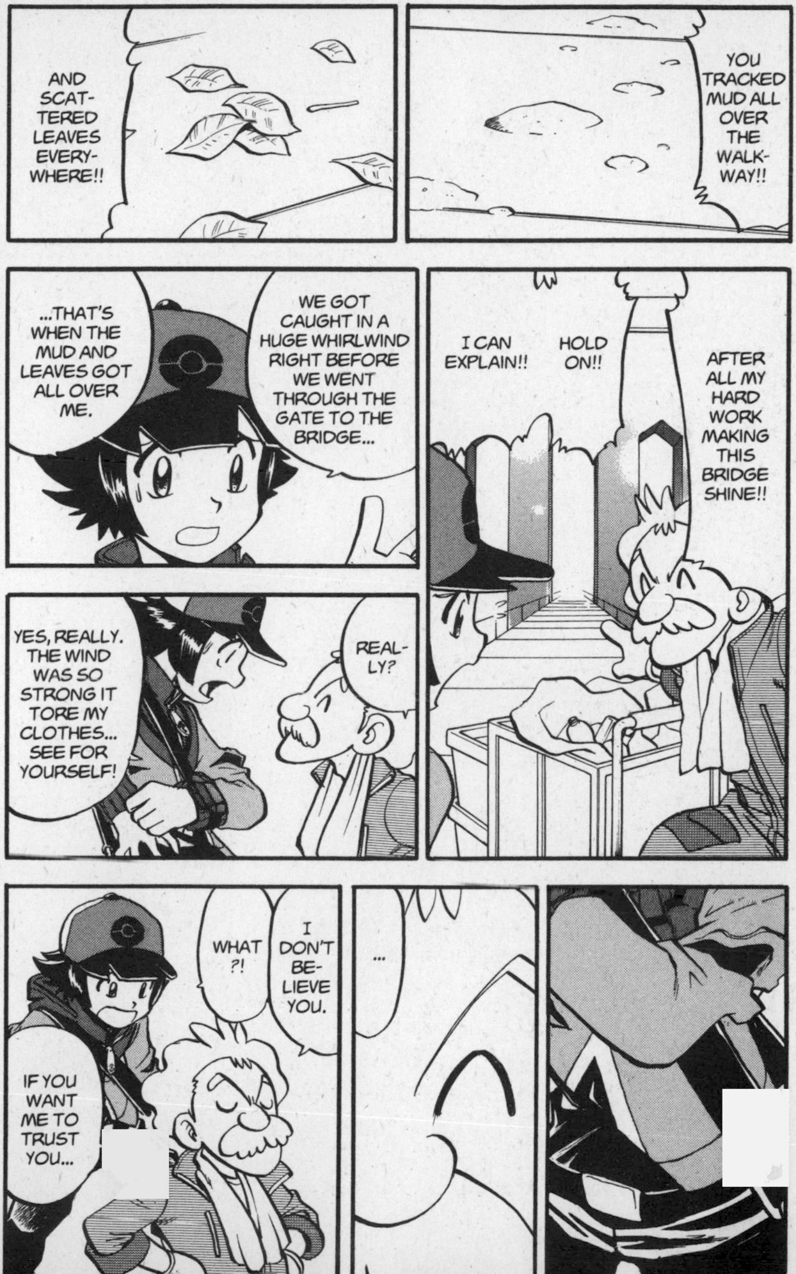
YOU TRACKED MUD ALL OVER THE WALKWAY!!
AND SCATTERED LEAVES EVERYWHERE!!
AFTER ALL MY HARD WORK MAKING THIS BRIDGE SHINE!!
HOLD ON!!
I CAN EXPLAIN!!
WE GOT CAUGHT IN A HUGE WHIRLWIND RIGHT BEFORE WE WENT THROUGH THE GATE TO THE BRIDGE...
...THAT'S WHEN THE MUD AND LEAVES GOT ALL OVER ME.
REALLY?
YES, REALLY. THE WIND WAS SO STRONG IT TORE MY CLOTHES... SEE FOR YOURSELF!
...
I DON'T BELIEVE YOU.
WHAT?!
IF YOU WANT ME TO TRUST YOU...

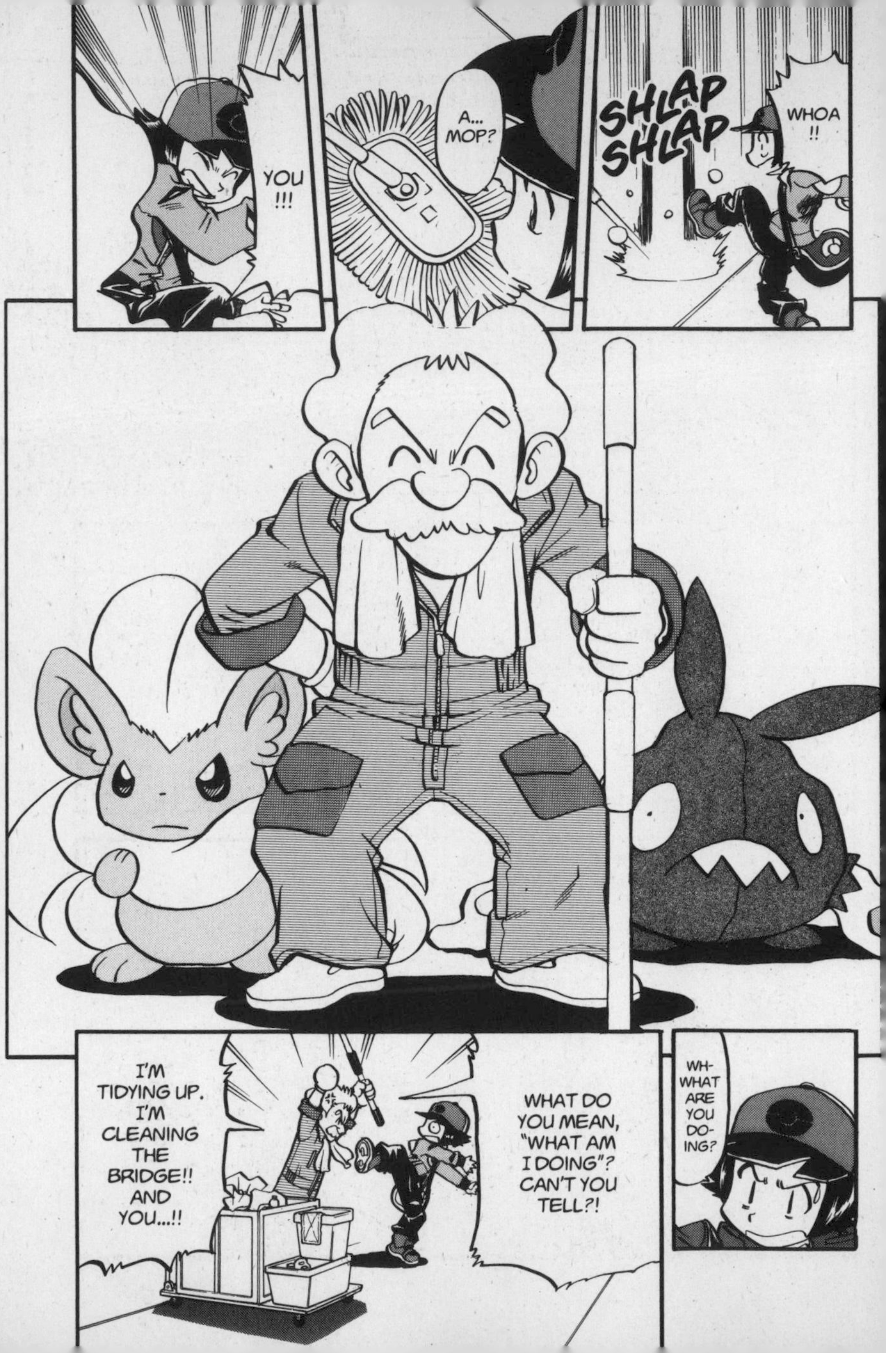
SHLAP SHLAP
WHOA!!
A... MOP?
YOU!!!
WH-WHAT ARE YOU DO-ING?
WHAT DO YOU MEAN, "WHAT AM I DOING"? CAN'T YOU TELL?!
I'M TIDYING UP. I'M CLEANING THE BRIDGE!! AND YOU...!!

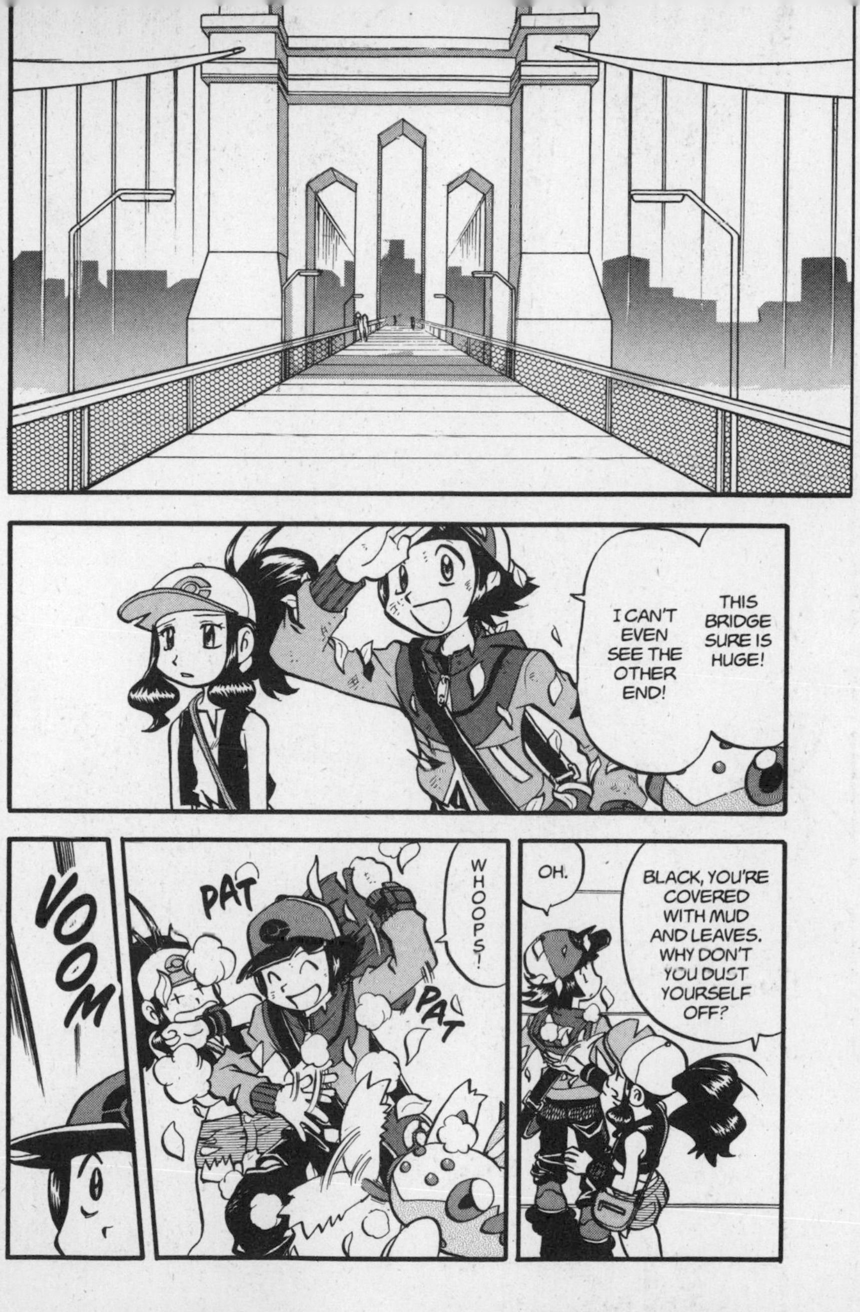
THIS BRIDGE SURE IS HUGE!
I CAN'T EVEN SEE THE OTHER END!
VOOM
PAT
WHOOPS!
PAT
OH.
BLACK, YOU'RE COVERED WITH MUD AND LEAVES. WHY DON'T YOU DUST YOURSELF OFF?

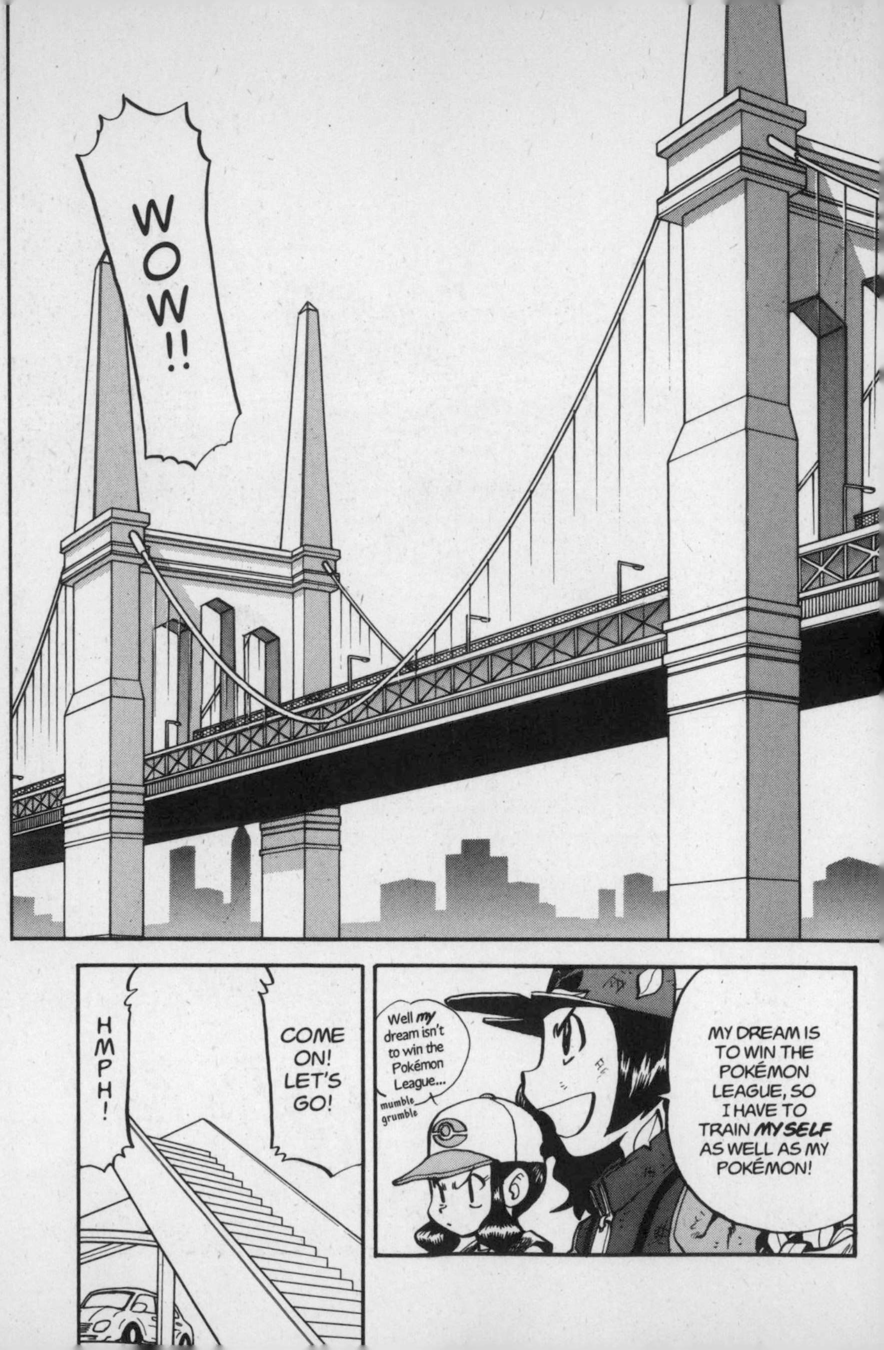
WOW!!
MY DREAM IS TO WIN THE POKÉMON LEAGUE, SO I HAVE TO TRAIN *MYSELF* AS WELL AS MY POKÉMON!
Well *my* dream isn't to win the Pokémon League...
mumble grumble
COME ON! LET'S GO!
HMPH!

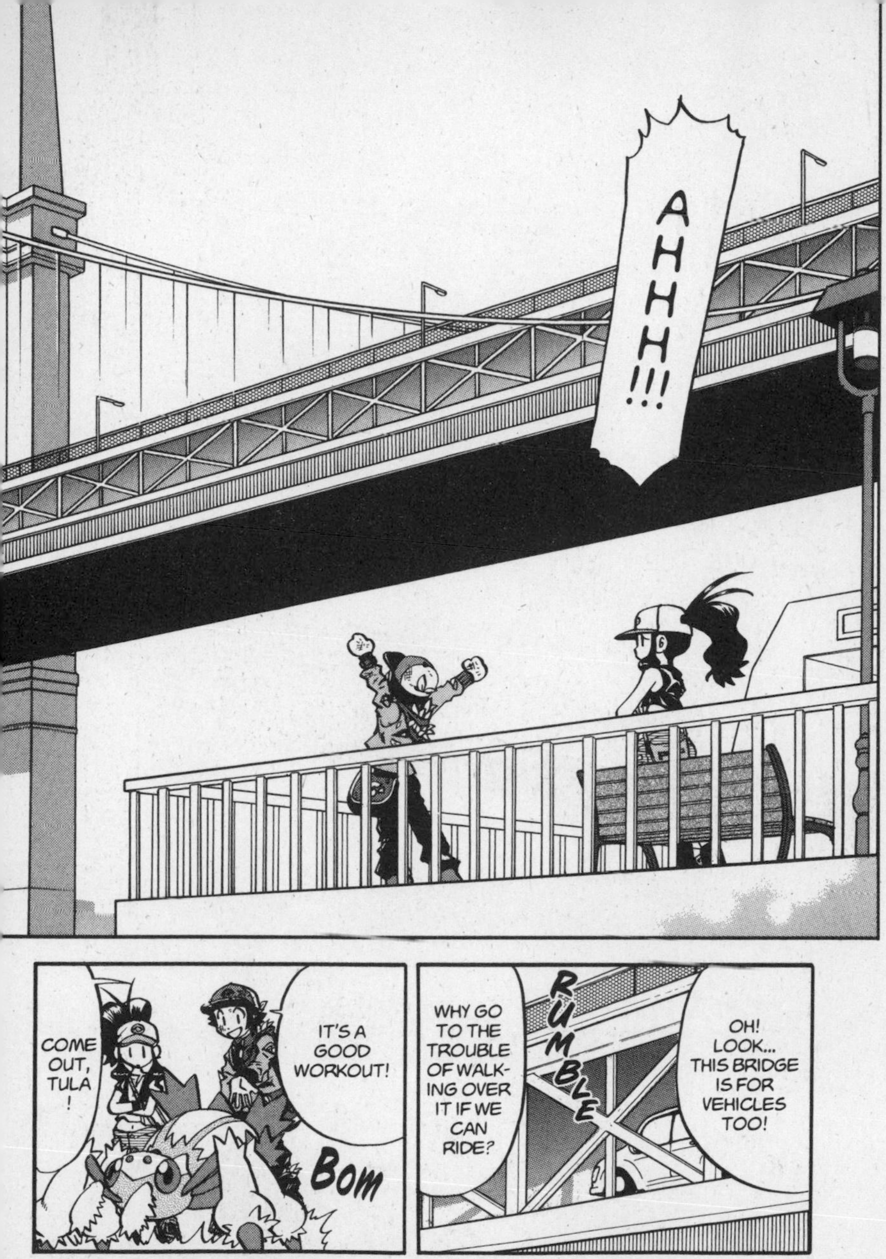
AHHH!!!
OH! LOOK... THIS BRIDGE IS FOR VEHICLES TOO!
RUMBLE
WHY GO TO THE TROUBLE OF WALK-ING OVER IT IF WE CAN RIDE?
IT'S A GOOD WORKOUT!
COME OUT, TULA!
BOM

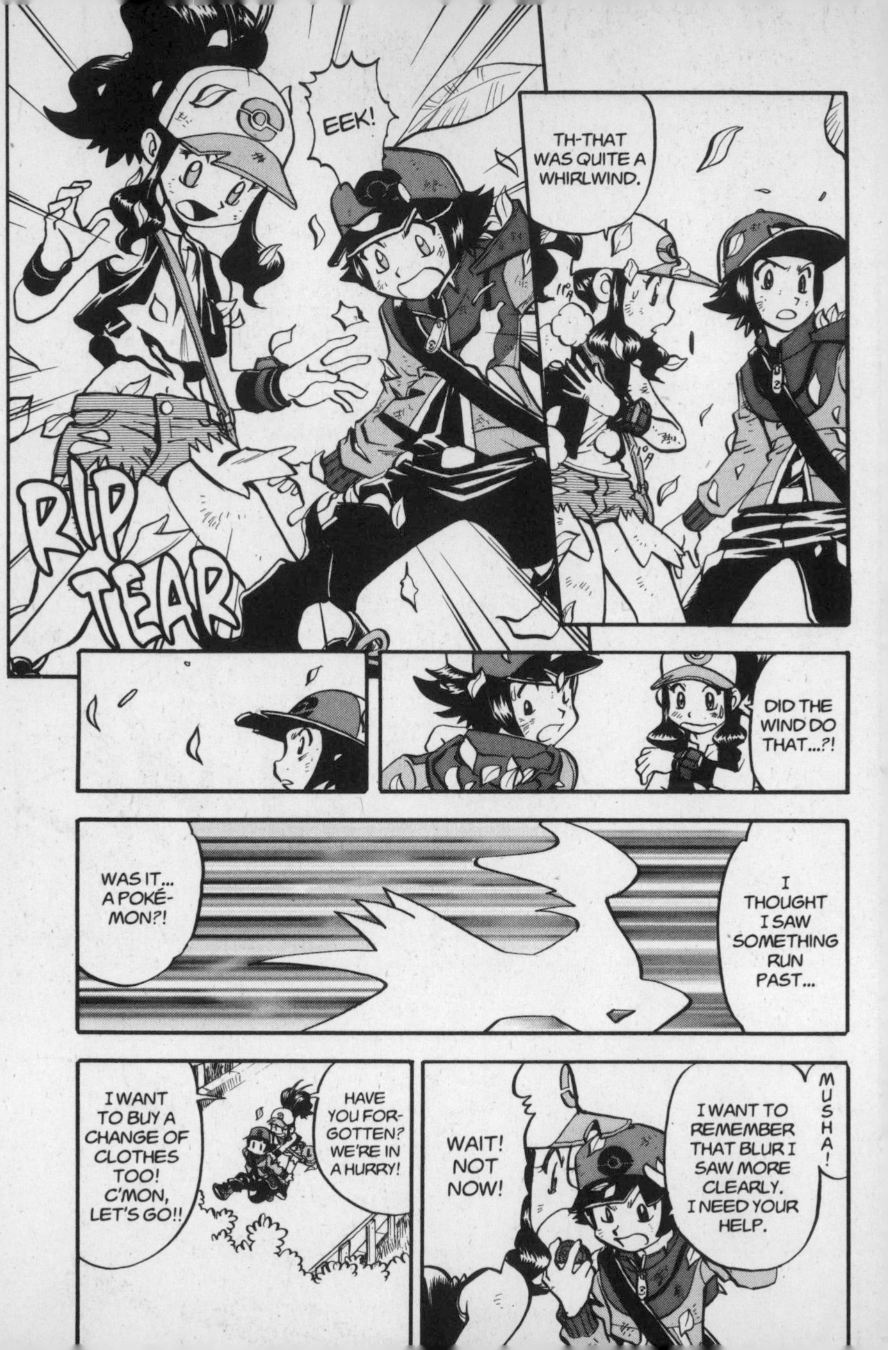
EEK!
RIP
TEAR
TH-THAT WAS QUITE A WHIRLWIND.
DID THE WIND DO THAT...?!
I THOUGHT I SAW SOMETHING RUN PAST...
WAS IT... A POKÉMON?!
MUSHA!
I WANT TO REMEMBER THAT BLUR I SAW MORE CLEARLY. I NEED YOUR HELP.
WAIT! NOT NOW!
HAVE YOU FORGOTTEN? WE'RE IN A HURRY!
I WANT TO BUY A CHANGE OF CLOTHES TOO! C'MON, LET'S GO!!

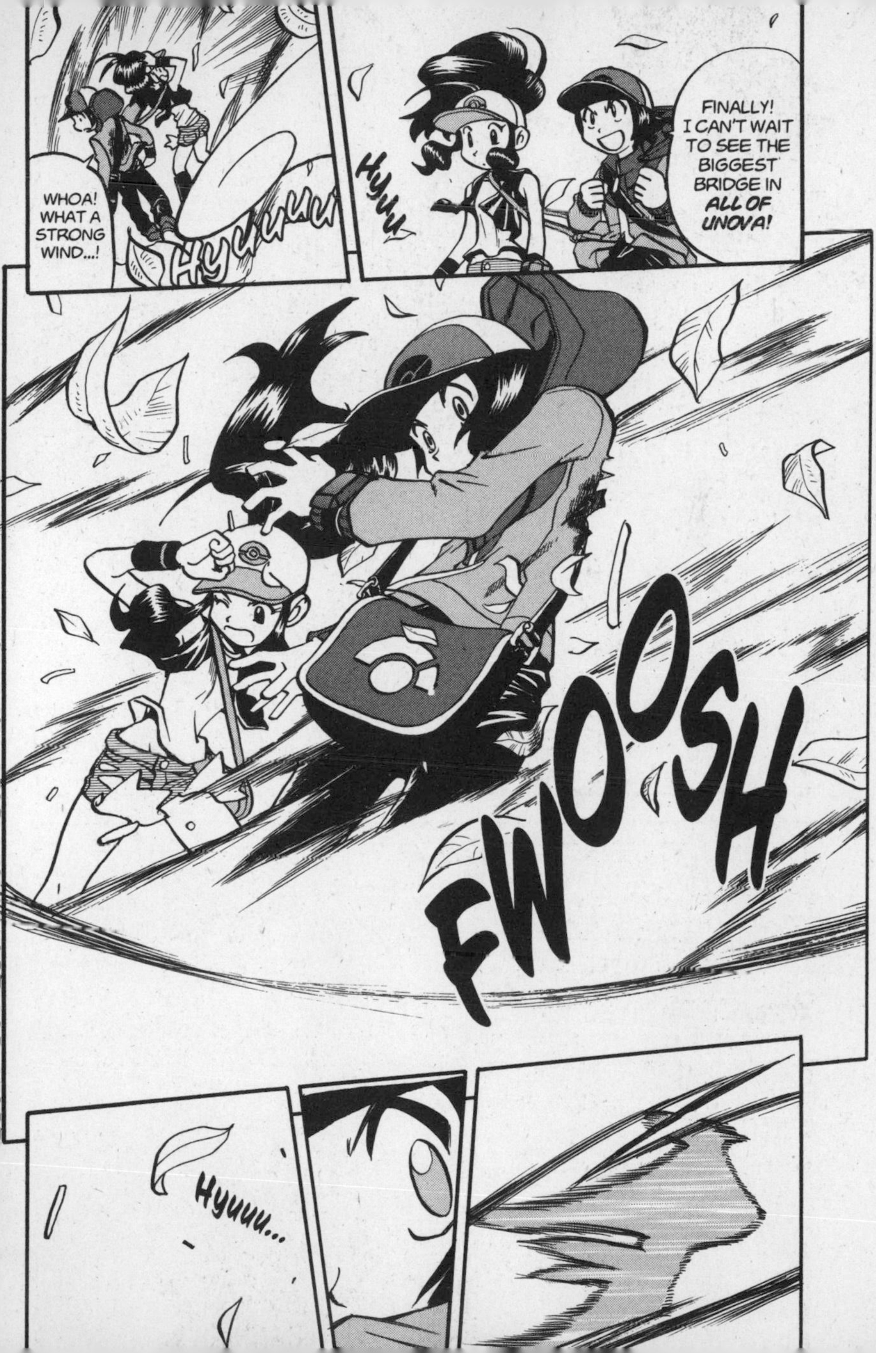
WHOA! WHAT A STRONG WIND...!
Hyuuuu
Hyuuu
FINALLY! I CAN'T WAIT TO SEE THE BIGGEST BRIDGE IN ALL OF UNOVA!
FWOOOSH
Hyuuu...

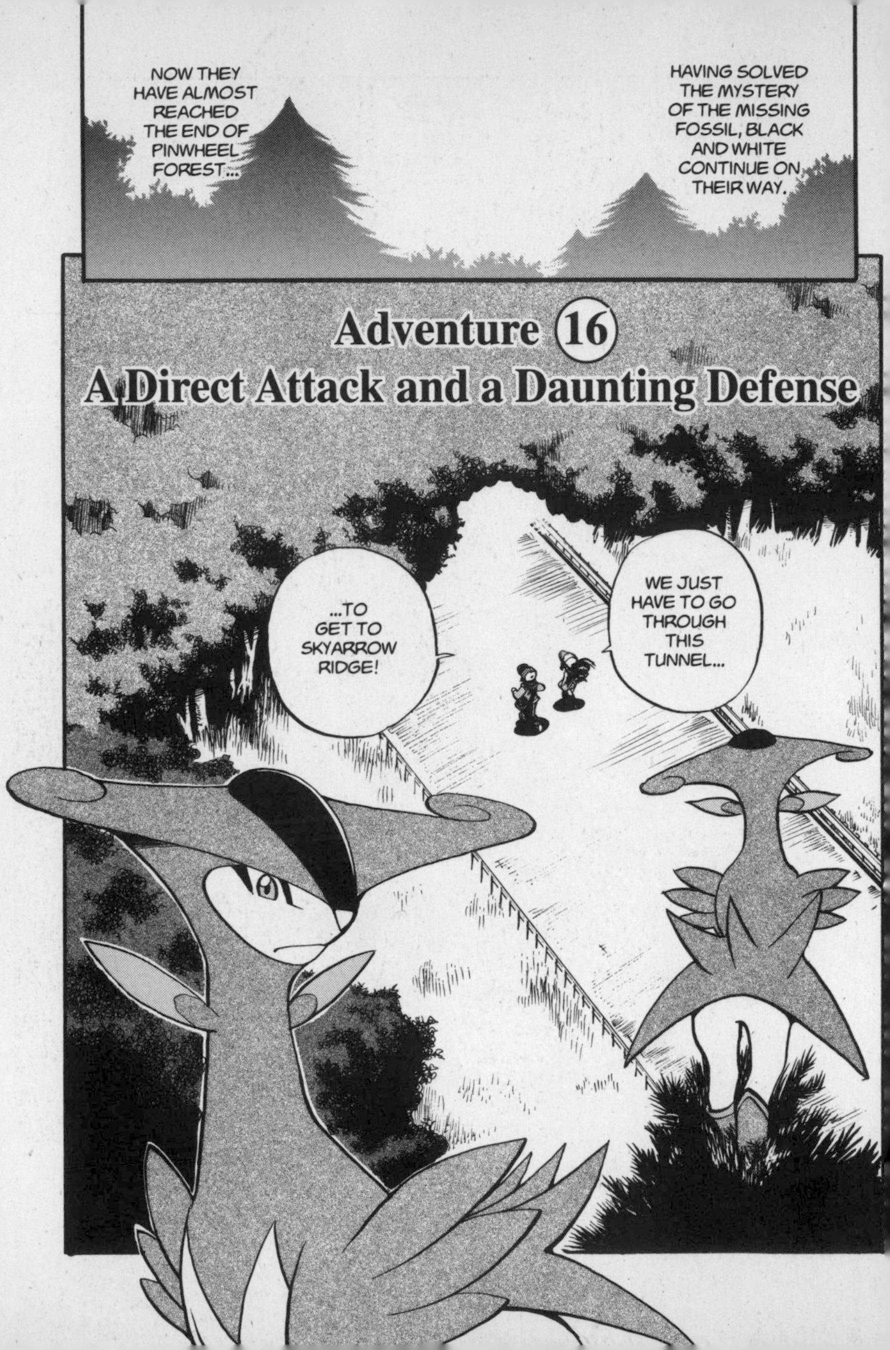
HAVING SOLVED THE MYSTERY OF THE MISSING FOSSIL, BLACK AND WHITE CONTINUE ON THEIR WAY.
NOW THEY HAVE ALMOST REACHED THE END OF PINWHEEL FOREST...
Adventure 16
A Direct Attack and a Daunting Defense
WE JUST HAVE TO GO THROUGH THIS TUNNEL...
...TO GET TO SKYARROW RIDGE!

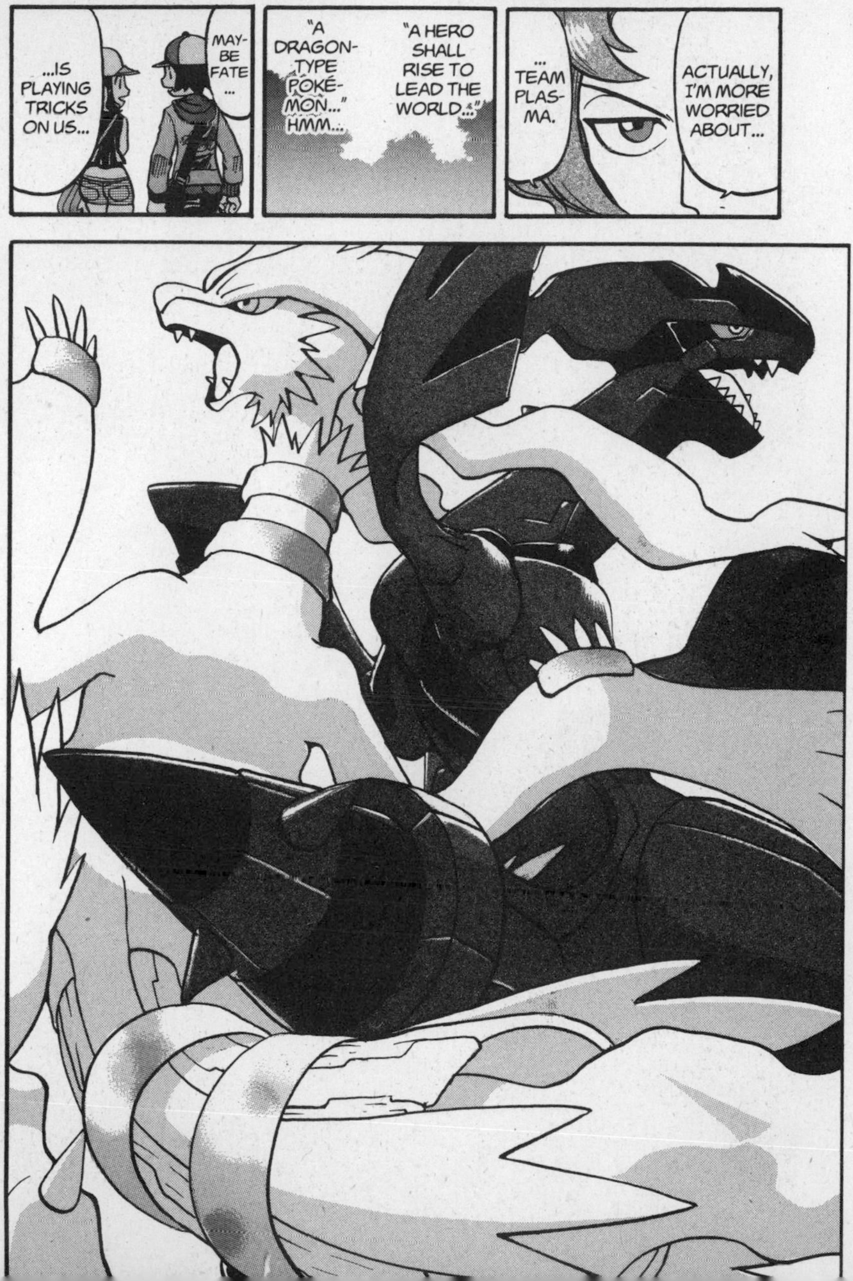
ACTUALLY, I'M MORE WORRIED ABOUT...
...TEAM PLASMA.
"A HERO SHALL RISE TO LEAD THE WORLD..."
"A DRAGON-TYPE POKÉMON..." HMM...
MAYBE FATE...
...IS PLAYING TRICKS ON US...

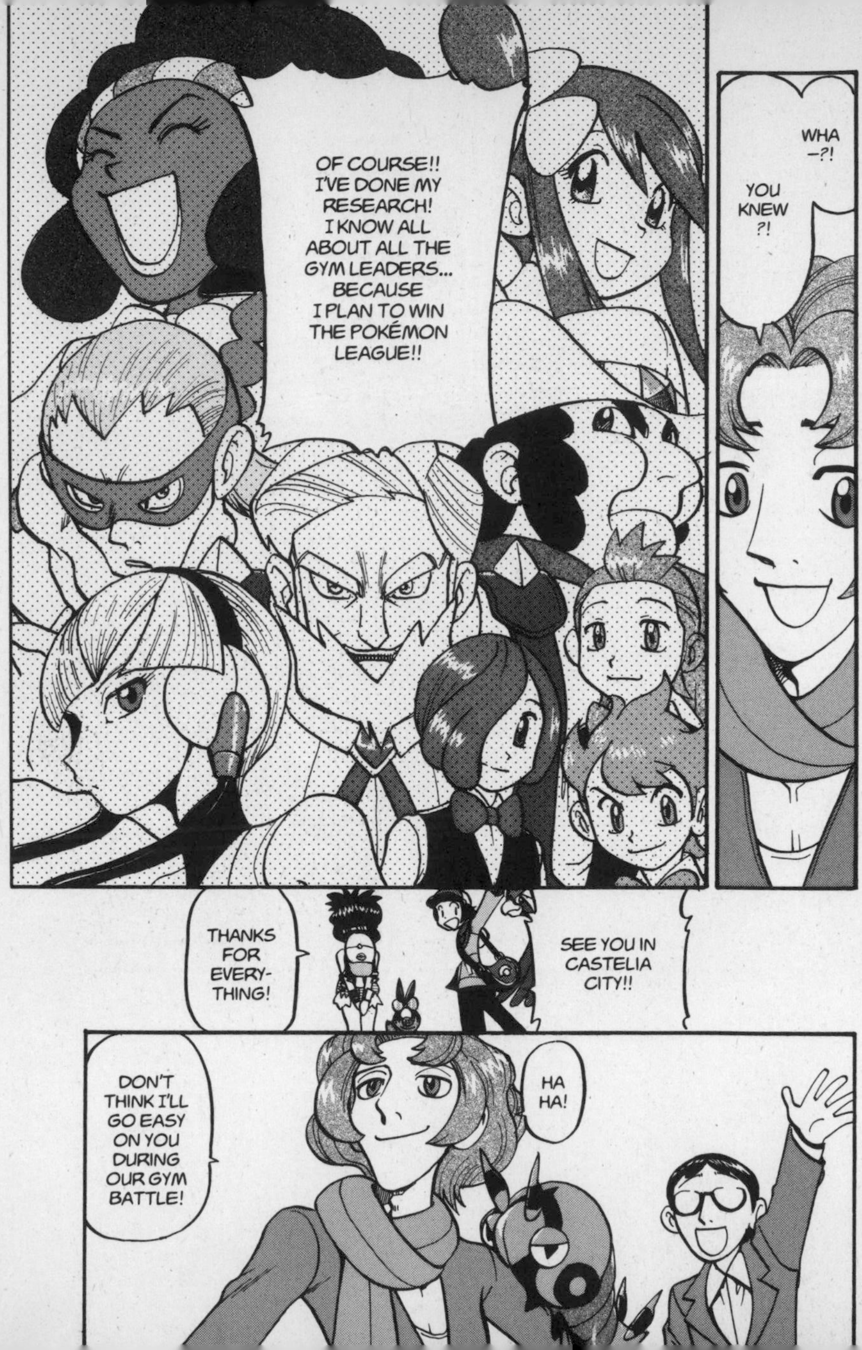
OF COURSE!! I'VE DONE MY RESEARCH! I KNOW ALL ABOUT ALL THE GYM LEADERS... BECAUSE I PLAN TO WIN THE POKÉMON LEAGUE!!
WHA–?!
YOU KNEW ?!
THANKS FOR EVERY-THING!
SEE YOU IN CASTELIA CITY!!
DON'T THINK I'LL GO EASY ON YOU DURING OUR GYM BATTLE!
HA HA!

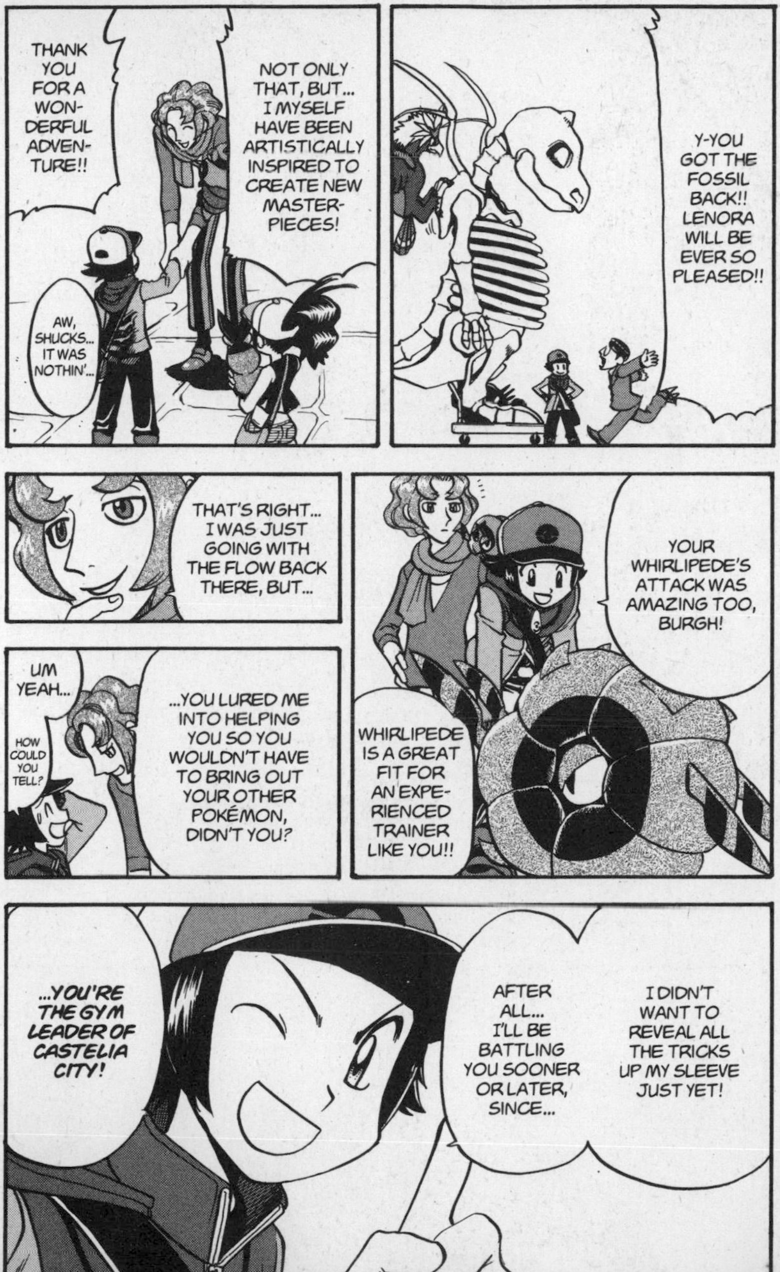
THANK YOU FOR A WON-DERFUL ADVEN-TURE!!
NOT ONLY THAT, BUT... I MYSELF HAVE BEEN ARTISTICALLY INSPIRED TO CREATE NEW MASTER-PIECES!
AW, SHUCKS... IT WAS NOTHIN'...
Y-YOU GOT THE FOSSIL BACK!! LENORA WILL BE EVER SO PLEASED!!
THAT'S RIGHT... I WAS JUST GOING WITH THE FLOW BACK THERE, BUT...
YOUR WHIRLIPEDE'S ATTACK WAS AMAZING TOO, BURGH!
WHIRLIPEDE IS A GREAT FIT FOR AN EXPE-RIENCED TRAINER LIKE YOU!!
...YOU LURED ME INTO HELPING YOU SO YOU WOULDN'T HAVE TO BRING OUT YOUR OTHER POKÉMON, DIDN'T YOU?
UM YEAH...
HOW COULD YOU TELL?
I DIDN'T WANT TO REVEAL ALL THE TRICKS UP MY SLEEVE JUST YET!
AFTER ALL... I'LL BE BATTLING YOU SOONER OR LATER, SINCE...
...YOU'RE THE GYM LEADER OF CASTELIA CITY!

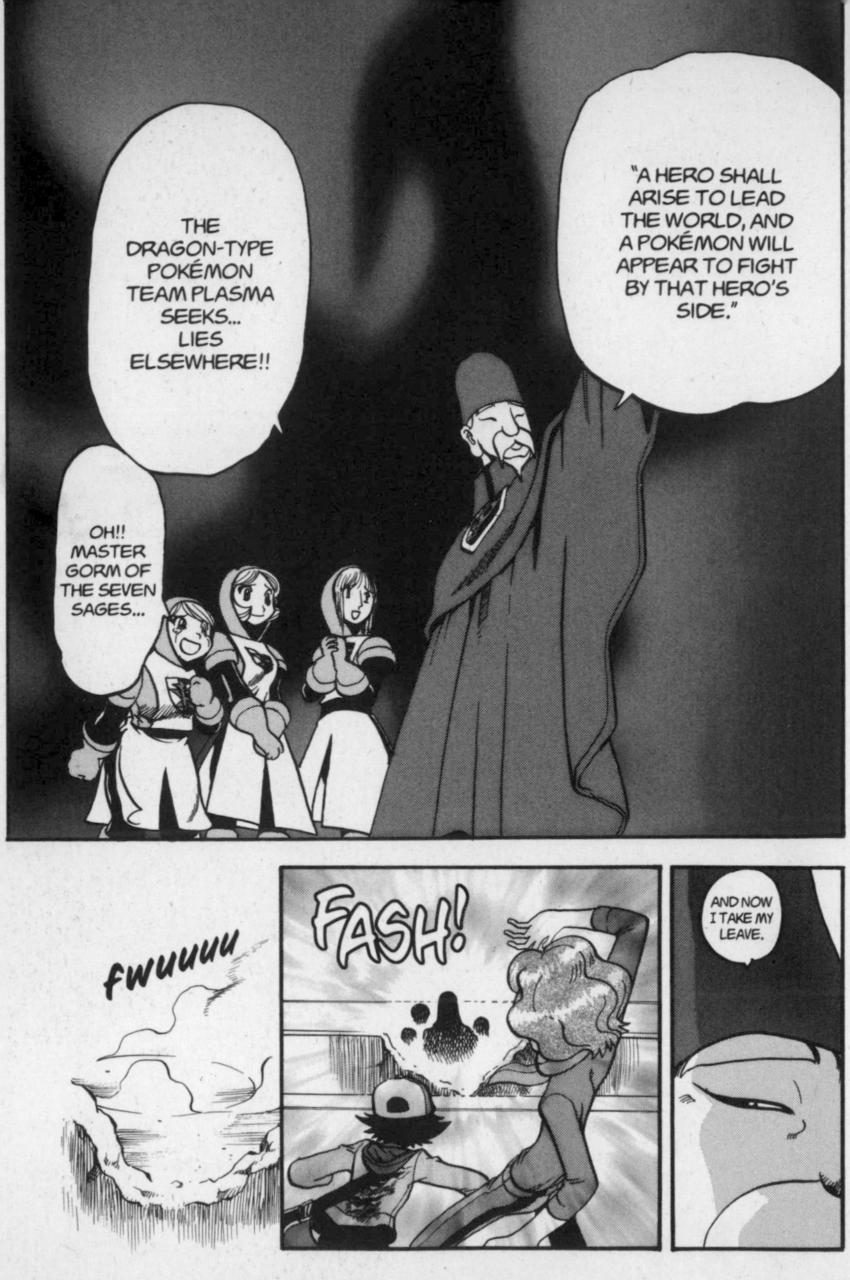
"A HERO SHALL ARISE TO LEAD THE WORLD, AND A POKÉMON WILL APPEAR TO FIGHT BY THAT HERO'S SIDE."
THE DRAGON-TYPE POKÉMON TEAM PLASMA SEEKS... LIES ELSEWHERE!!
OH!! MASTER GORM OF THE SEVEN SAGES...
AND NOW I TAKE MY LEAVE.
FASH!
FWUUUU

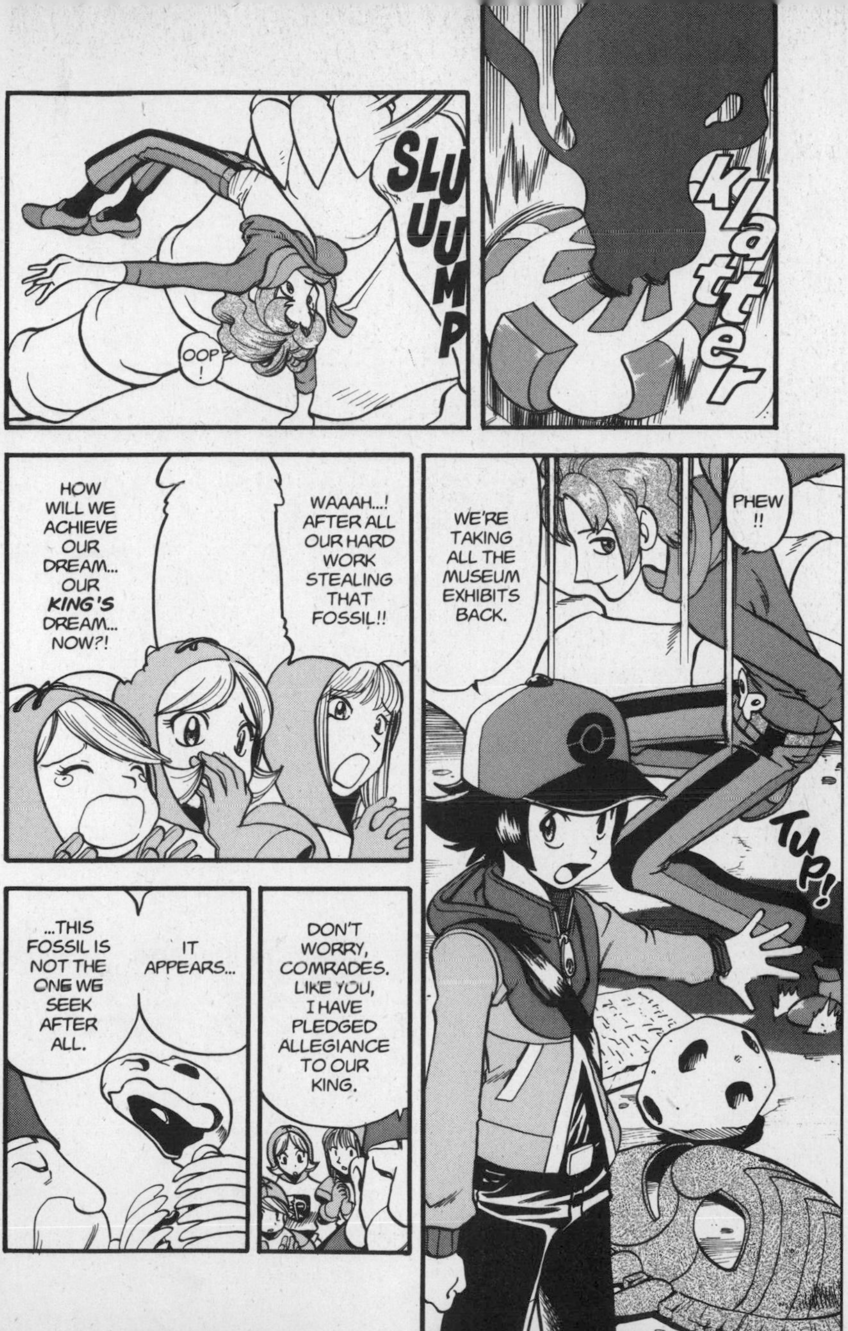
SLUUUMP
OOP!
klatter
HOW WILL WE ACHIEVE OUR DREAM... OUR **KING'S** DREAM... NOW?!
WAAAH...! AFTER ALL OUR HARD WORK STEALING THAT FOSSIL!!
WE'RE TAKING ALL THE MUSEUM EXHIBITS BACK.
PHEW!!
TUP!
IT APPEARS...
...THIS FOSSIL IS NOT THE ONE WE SEEK AFTER ALL.
DON'T WORRY, COMRADES. LIKE YOU, I HAVE PLEDGED ALLEGIANCE TO OUR KING.

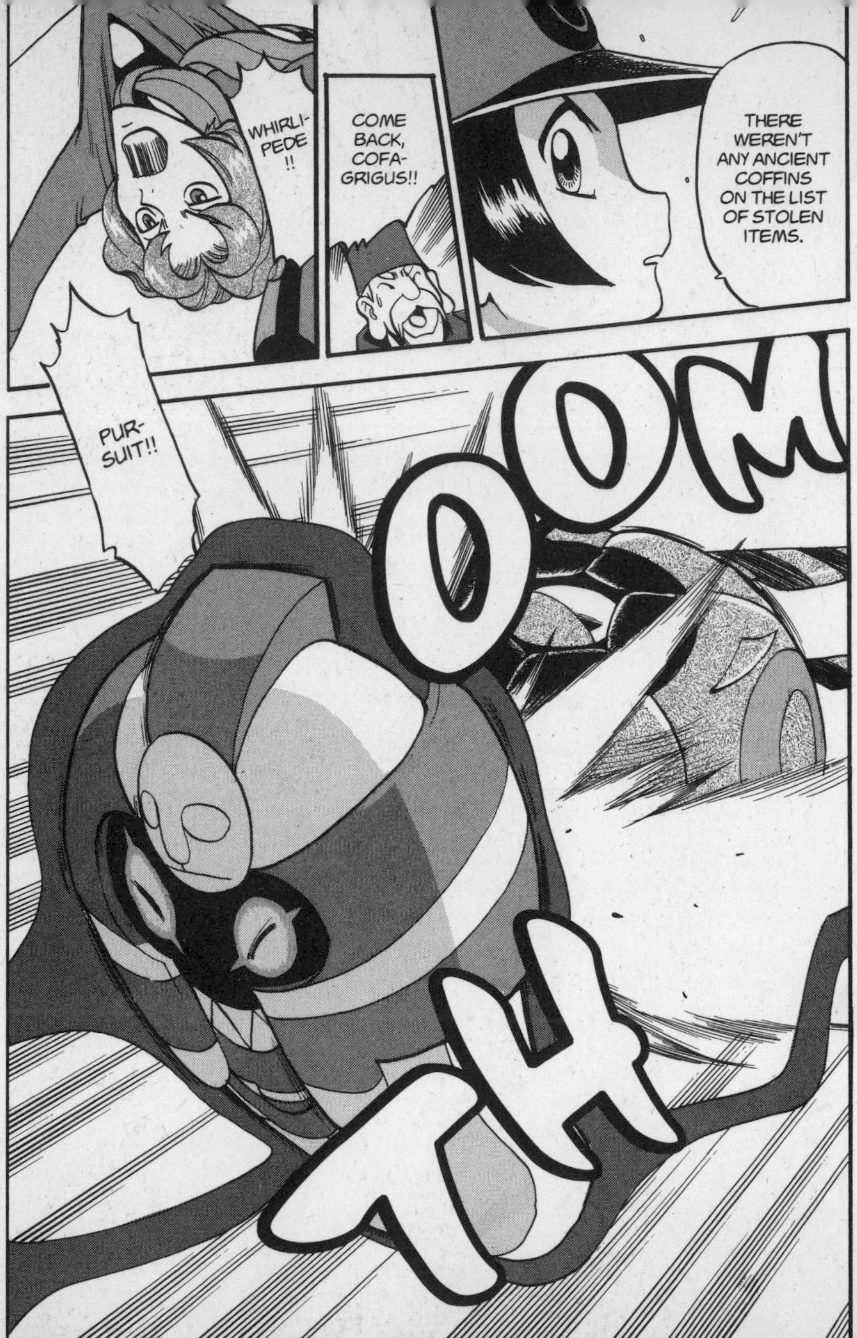
THERE WEREN'T ANY ANCIENT COFFINS ON THE LIST OF STOLEN ITEMS.
COME BACK, COFA-GRIGUS!!
WHIRLI-PEDE !!
PUR-SUIT!!
THOOM

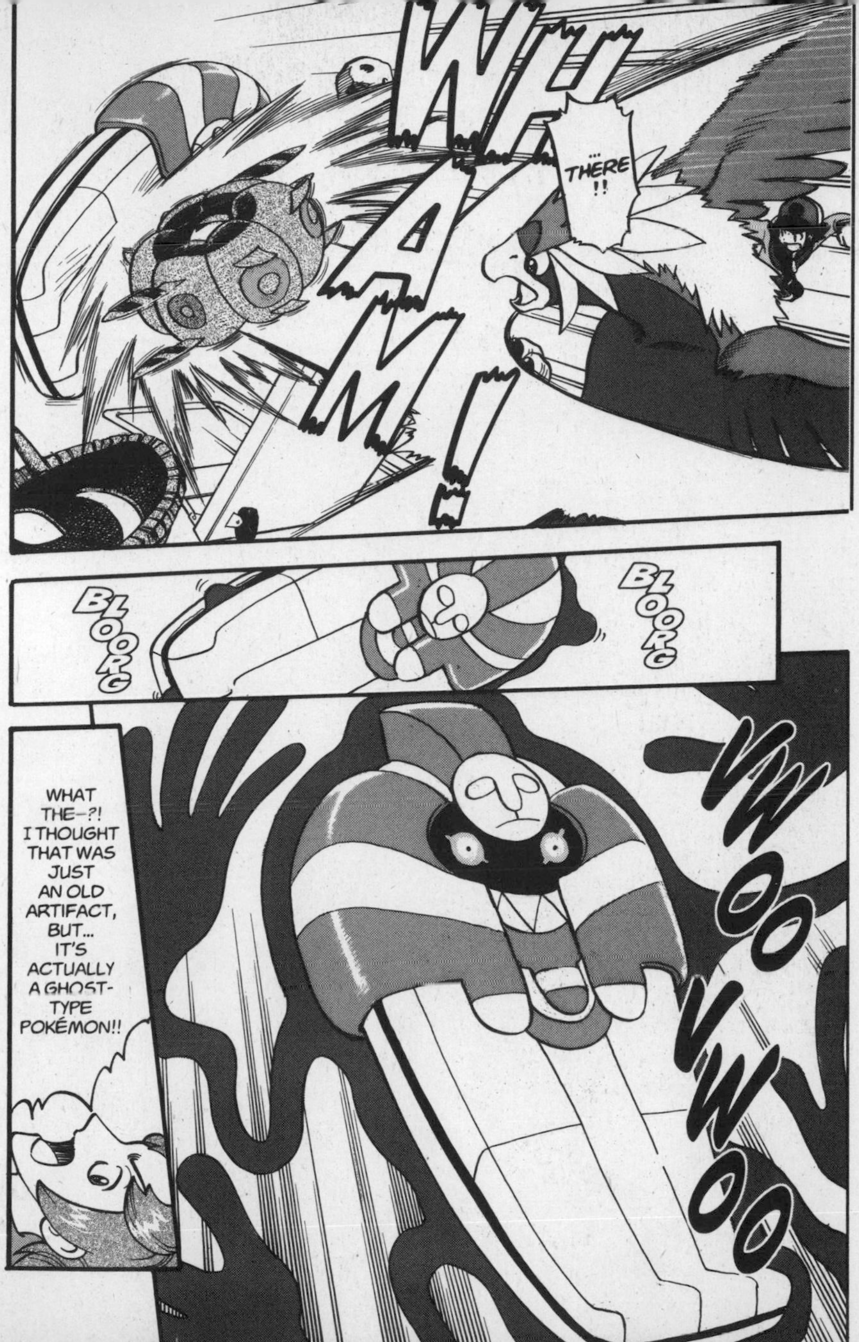
WHAM!
...THERE!!
BLOORG BLOORG
VWOO VWOO VWOO
WHAT THE--?! I THOUGHT THAT WAS JUST AN OLD ARTIFACT, BUT... IT'S ACTUALLY A GHOST-TYPE POKÉMON!!

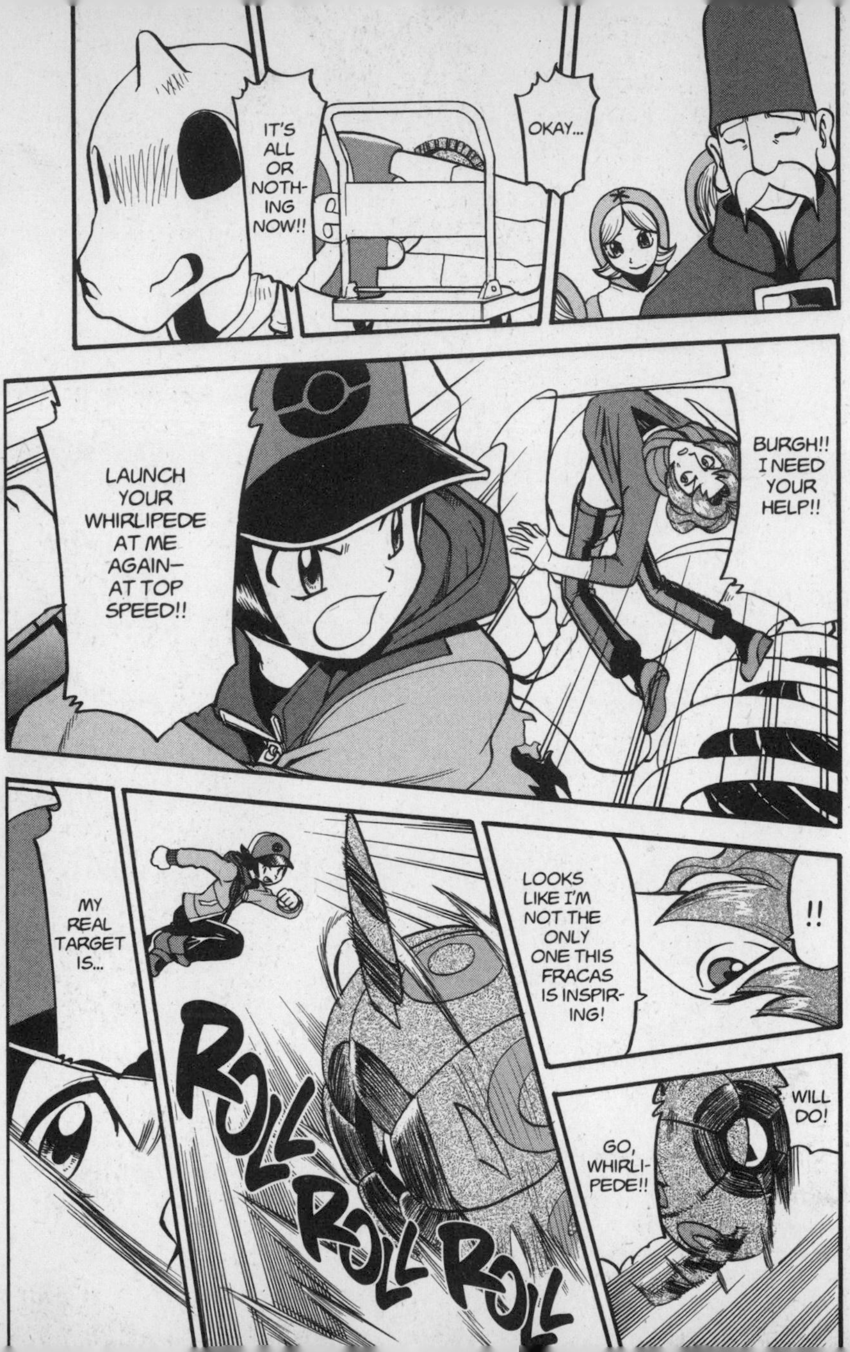
IT'S ALL OR NOTHING NOW!!
OKAY...
BURGH!! I NEED YOUR HELP!!
LAUNCH YOUR WHIRLIPEDE AT ME AGAIN—AT TOP SPEED!!
MY REAL TARGET IS...
ROLL ROLL ROLL
LOOKS LIKE I'M NOT THE ONLY ONE THIS FRACAS IS INSPIRING!
!!
GO, WHIRLIPEDE!!
WILL DO!

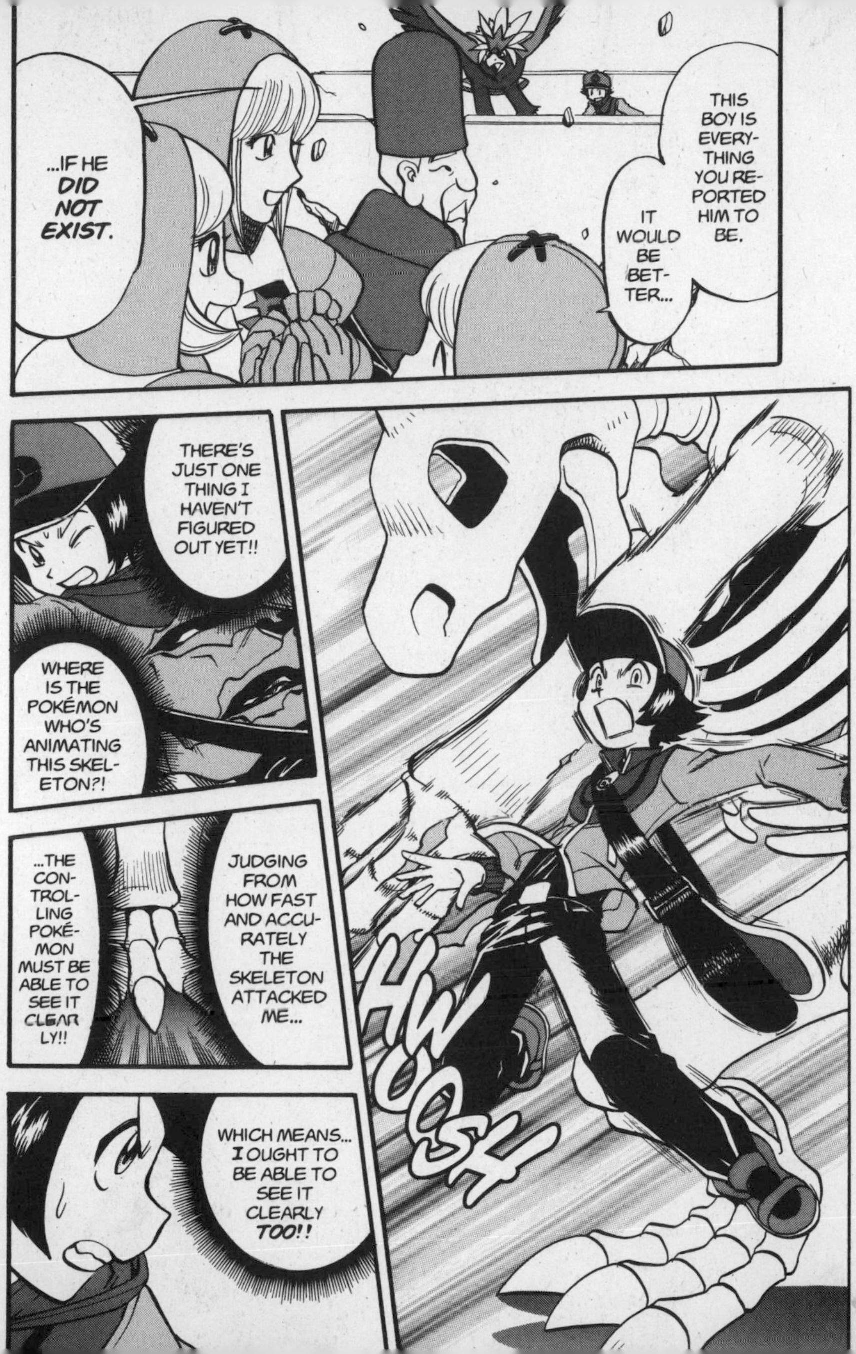
THIS BOY IS EVERYTHING YOU REPORTED HIM TO BE.
IT WOULD BE BETTER...
...IF HE DID NOT EXIST.
WHOOSH
THERE'S JUST ONE THING I HAVEN'T FIGURED OUT YET!!
WHERE IS THE POKÉMON WHO'S ANIMATING THIS SKELETON?!
JUDGING FROM HOW FAST AND ACCURATELY THE SKELETON ATTACKED ME...
...THE CONTROLLING POKÉMON MUST BE ABLE TO SEE IT CLEARLY!!
WHICH MEANS... I OUGHT TO BE ABLE TO SEE IT CLEARLY TOO!!

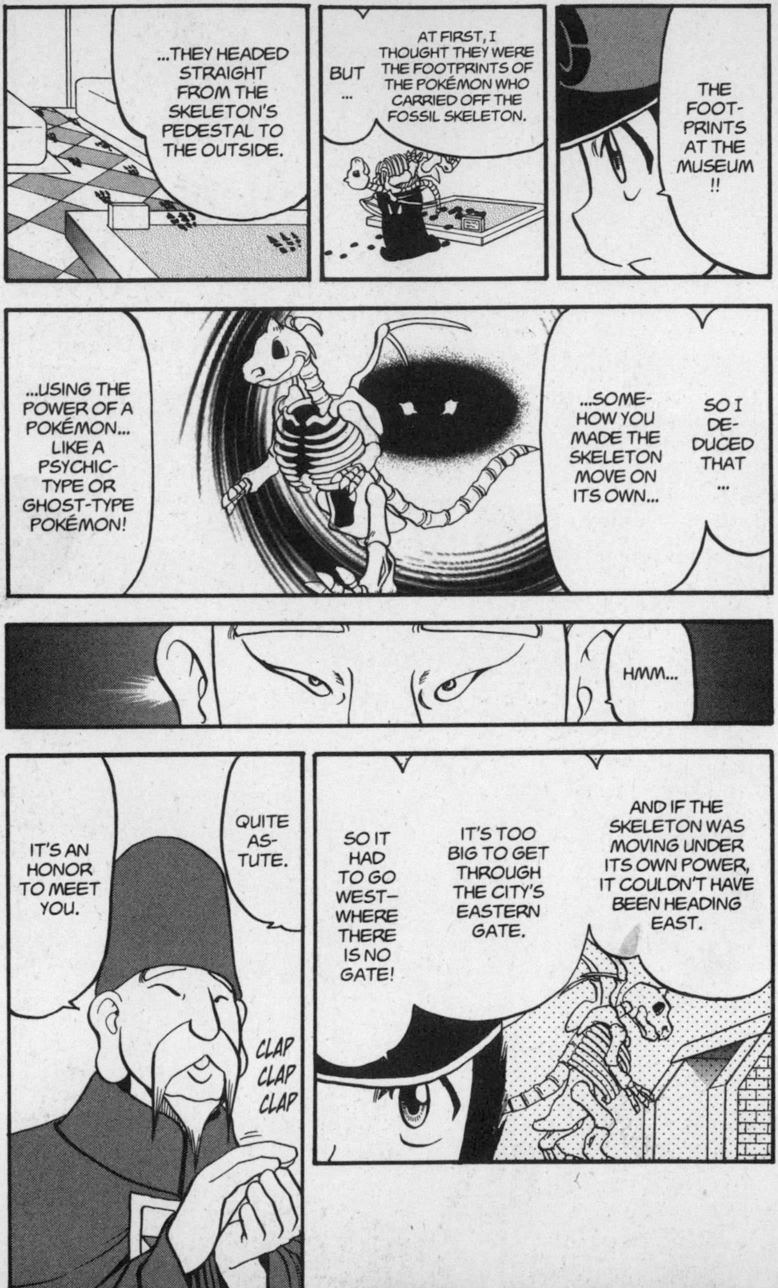
THE FOOT-PRINTS AT THE MUSEUM !!
AT FIRST, I THOUGHT THEY WERE THE FOOTPRINTS OF THE POKÉMON WHO CARRIED OFF THE FOSSIL SKELETON.
BUT ...
...THEY HEADED STRAIGHT FROM THE SKELETON'S PEDESTAL TO THE OUTSIDE.
SO I DE-DUCED THAT ...
...SOME-HOW YOU MADE THE SKELETON MOVE ON ITS OWN...
...USING THE POWER OF A POKÉMON... LIKE A PSYCHIC-TYPE OR GHOST-TYPE POKÉMON!
HMM...
AND IF THE SKELETON WAS MOVING UNDER ITS OWN POWER, IT COULDN'T HAVE BEEN HEADING EAST.
IT'S TOO BIG TO GET THROUGH THE CITY'S EASTERN GATE.
SO IT HAD TO GO WEST-WHERE THERE IS NO GATE!
QUITE AS-TUTE.
CLAP CLAP CLAP
IT'S AN HONOR TO MEET YOU.

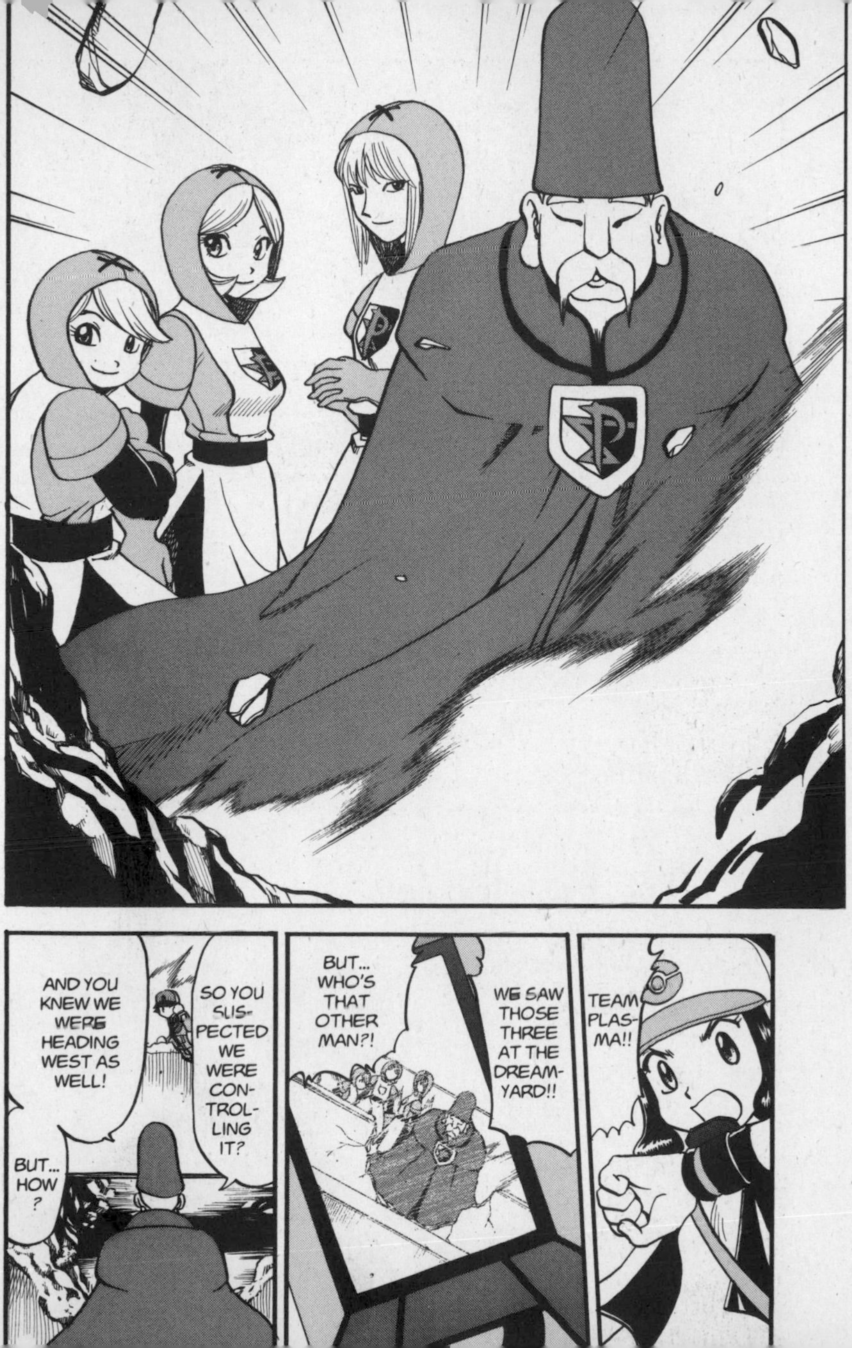
TEAM PLASMA!!
WE SAW THOSE THREE AT THE DREAMYARD!!
BUT... WHO'S THAT OTHER MAN?!
SO YOU SUSPECTED WE WERE CONTROLLING IT?
AND YOU KNEW WE WERE HEADING WEST AS WELL!
BUT... HOW?

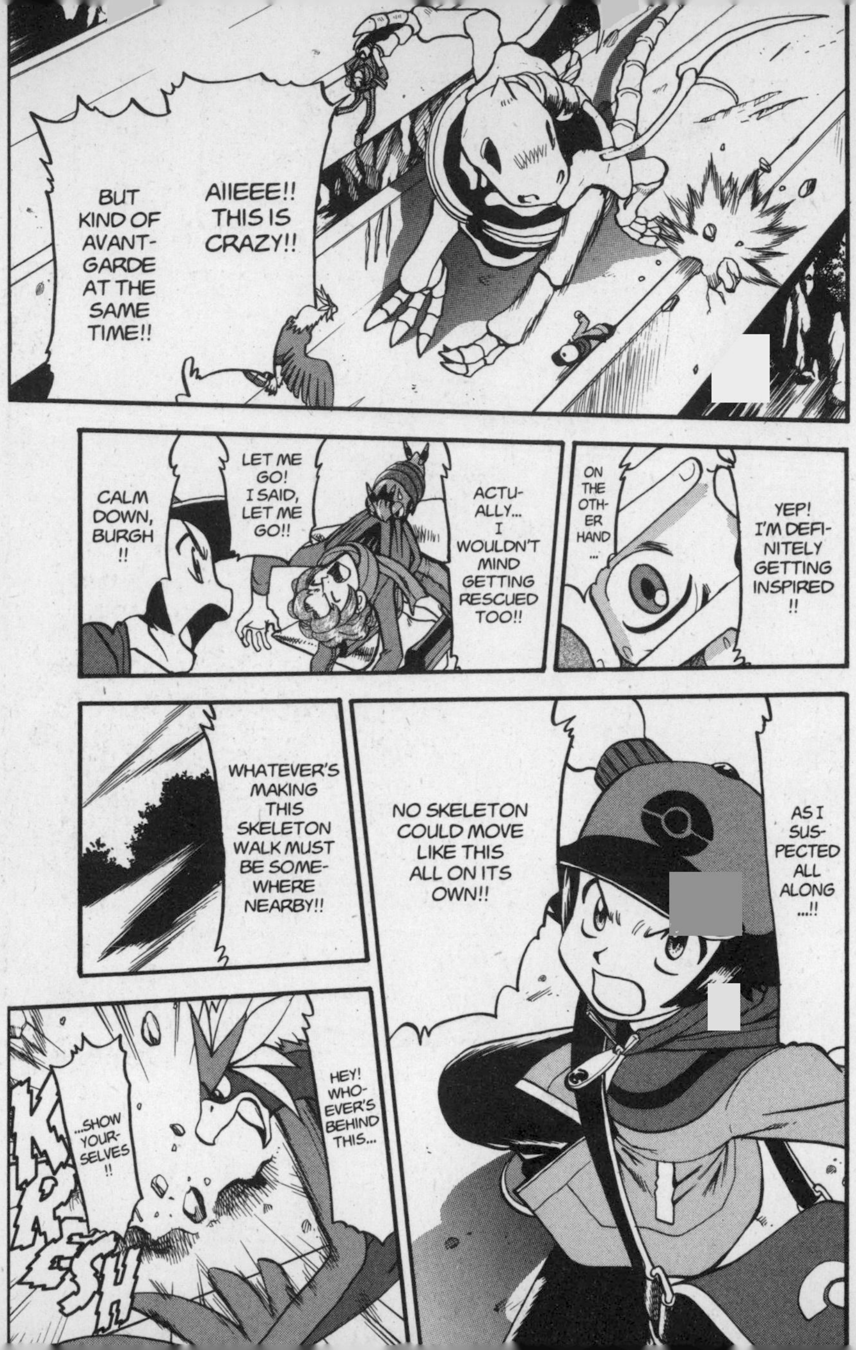
AIIEEE!! THIS IS CRAZY!!
BUT KIND OF AVANT-GARDE AT THE SAME TIME!!
YEP! I'M DEFINITELY GETTING INSPIRED!!
ON THE OTHER HAND...
ACTUALLY... I WOULDN'T MIND GETTING RESCUED TOO!!
LET ME GO! I SAID, LET ME GO!!
CALM DOWN, BURGH!!
AS I SUSPECTED ALL ALONG...!!
NO SKELETON COULD MOVE LIKE THIS ALL ON ITS OWN!!
WHATEVER'S MAKING THIS SKELETON WALK MUST BE SOMEWHERE NEARBY!!
HEY! WHOEVER'S BEHIND THIS...
...SHOW YOURSELVES!!
KRSH

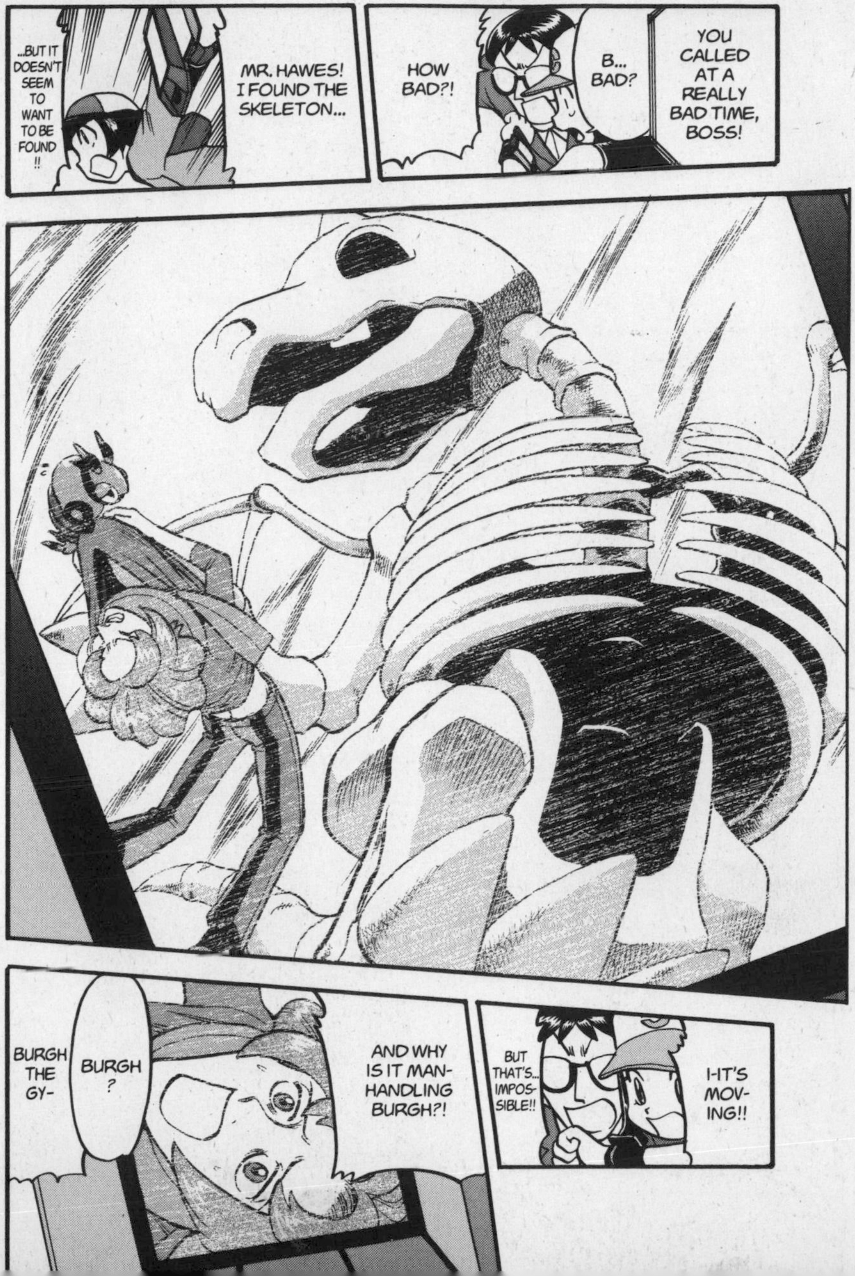
YOU CALLED AT A REALLY BAD TIME, BOSS!
B... BAD?
HOW BAD?!
MR. HAWES! I FOUND THE SKELETON...
...BUT IT DOESN'T SEEM TO WANT TO BE FOUND!!
I-IT'S MOVING!!
BUT THAT'S... IMPOSSIBLE!!
AND WHY IS IT MAN-HANDLING BURGH?!
BURGH?
BURGH THE GY-

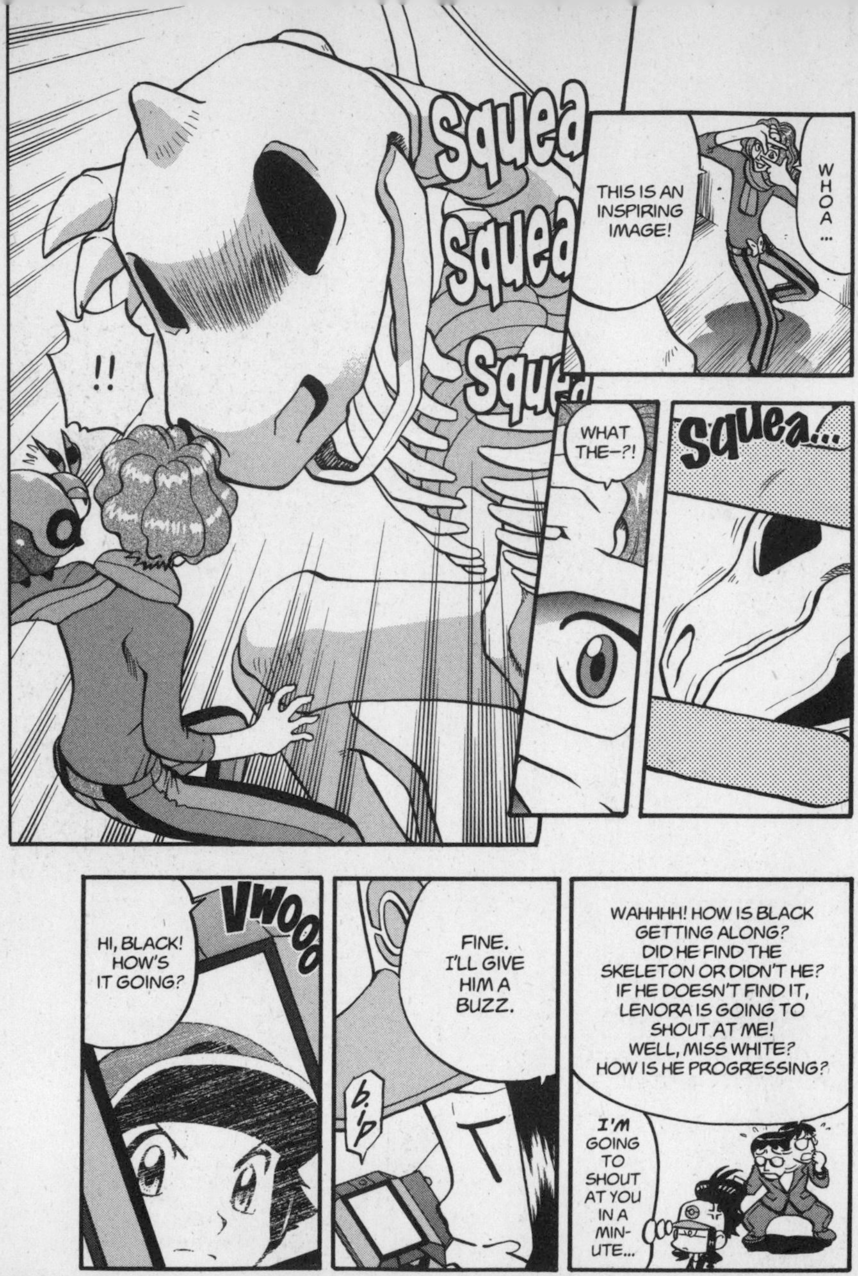

!!
Squea
Squea
Squea
WHOA...
THIS IS AN INSPIRING IMAGE!
WHAT THE--?!
Squea...
HI, BLACK! HOW'S IT GOING?
VWOOO
FINE. I'LL GIVE HIM A BUZZ.
b.i.p
WAHHHH! HOW IS BLACK GETTING ALONG? DID HE FIND THE SKELETON OR DIDN'T HE? IF HE DOESN'T FIND IT, LENORA IS GOING TO SHOUT AT ME! WELL, MISS WHITE? HOW IS HE PROGRESSING?
I'M GOING TO SHOUT AT YOU IN A MIN-UTE...

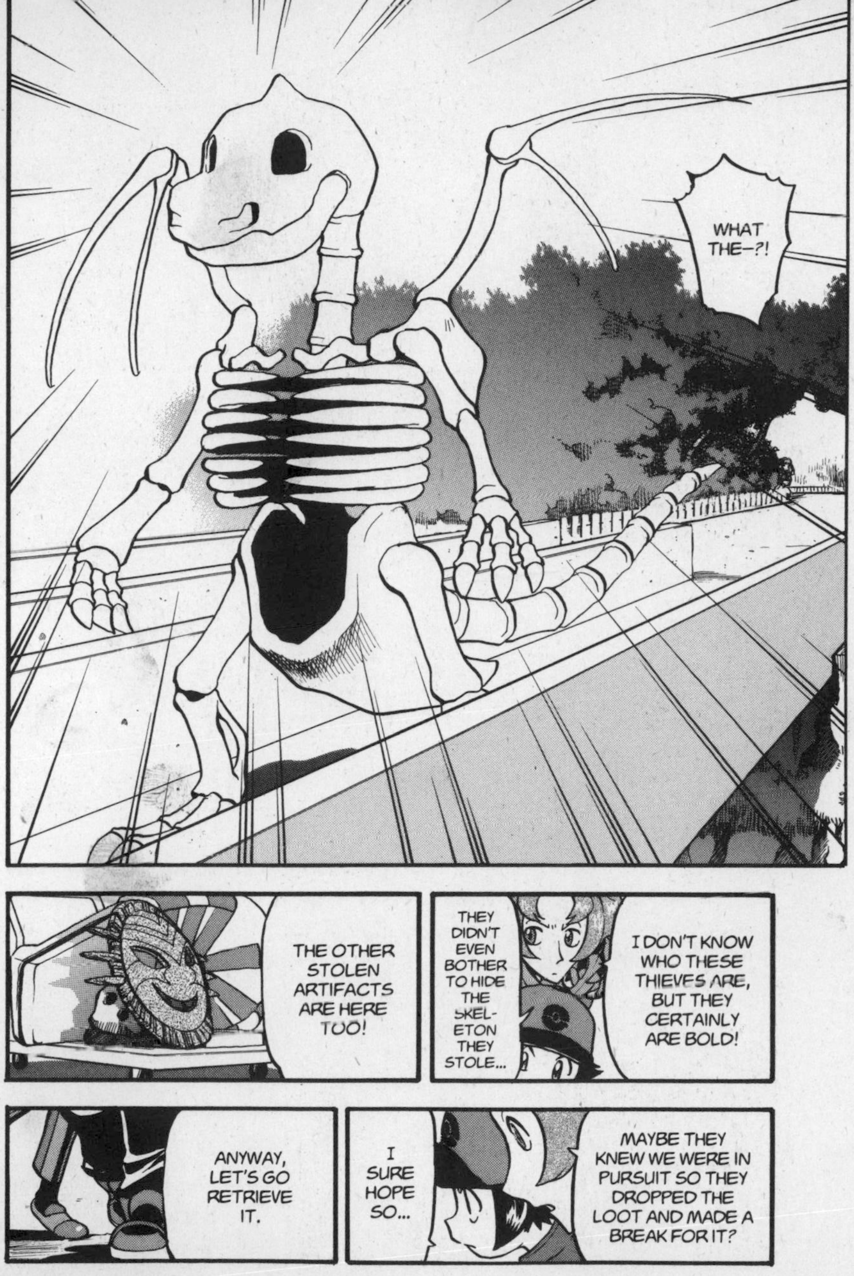
WHAT THE–?!
I DON'T KNOW WHO THESE THIEVES ARE, BUT THEY CERTAINLY ARE BOLD!
THEY DIDN'T EVEN BOTHER TO HIDE THE SKEL-ETON THEY STOLE...
THE OTHER STOLEN ARTIFACTS ARE HERE TOO!
MAYBE THEY KNEW WE WERE IN PURSUIT SO THEY DROPPED THE LOOT AND MADE A BREAK FOR IT?
I SURE HOPE SO...
ANYWAY, LET'S GO RETRIEVE IT.

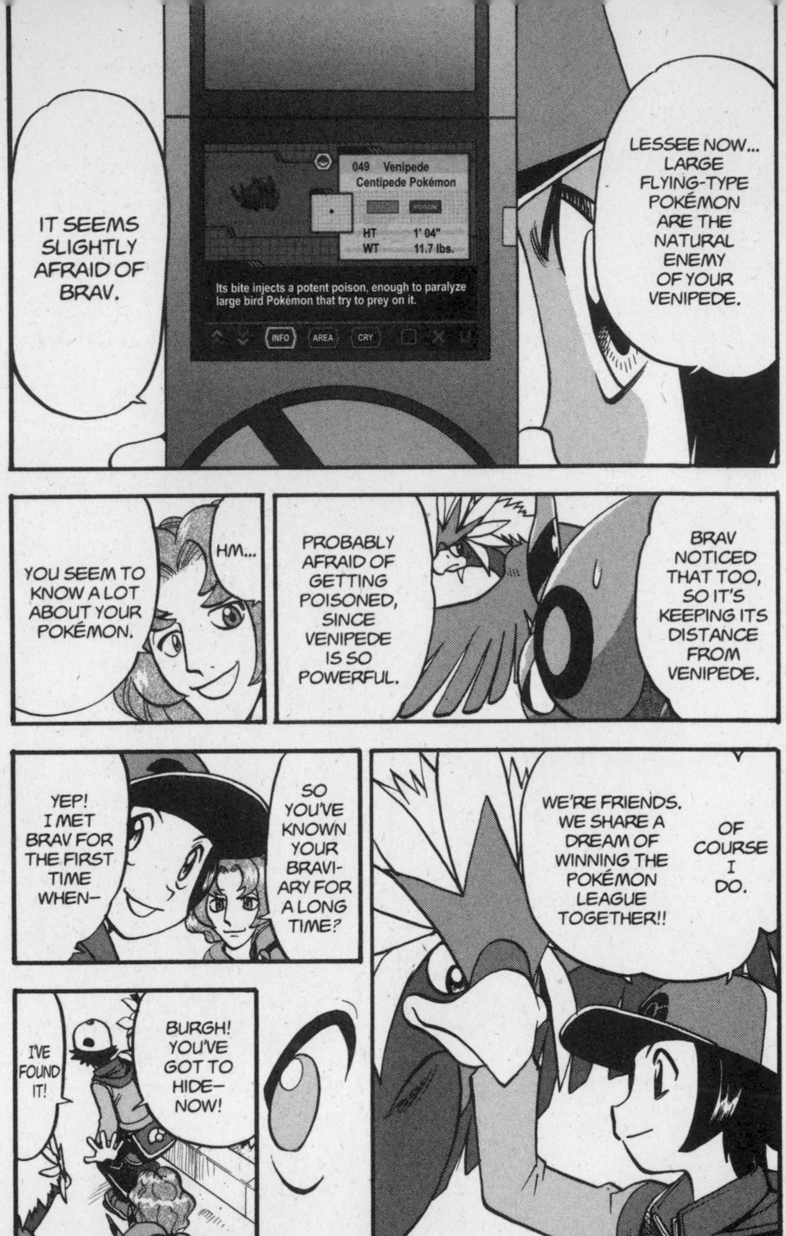

IT SEEMS SLIGHTLY AFRAID OF BRAV.
049 Venipede
Centipede Pokémon
POISON
HT 1' 04"
WT 11.7 lbs.
Its bite injects a potent poison, enough to paralyze large bird Pokémon that try to prey on it.
INFO
AREA
CRY
LESSEE NOW... LARGE FLYING-TYPE POKÉMON ARE THE NATURAL ENEMY OF YOUR VENIPEDE.
YOU SEEM TO KNOW A LOT ABOUT YOUR POKÉMON.
HM...
PROBABLY AFRAID OF GETTING POISONED, SINCE VENIPEDE IS SO POWERFUL.
BRAV NOTICED THAT TOO, SO IT'S KEEPING ITS DISTANCE FROM VENIPEDE.
YEP! I MET BRAV FOR THE FIRST TIME WHEN—
SO YOU'VE KNOWN YOUR BRAVIARY FOR A LONG TIME?
WE'RE FRIENDS. WE SHARE A DREAM OF WINNING THE POKÉMON LEAGUE TOGETHER!!
OF COURSE I DO.
I'VE FOUND IT!
BURGH! YOU'VE GOT TO HIDE—NOW!

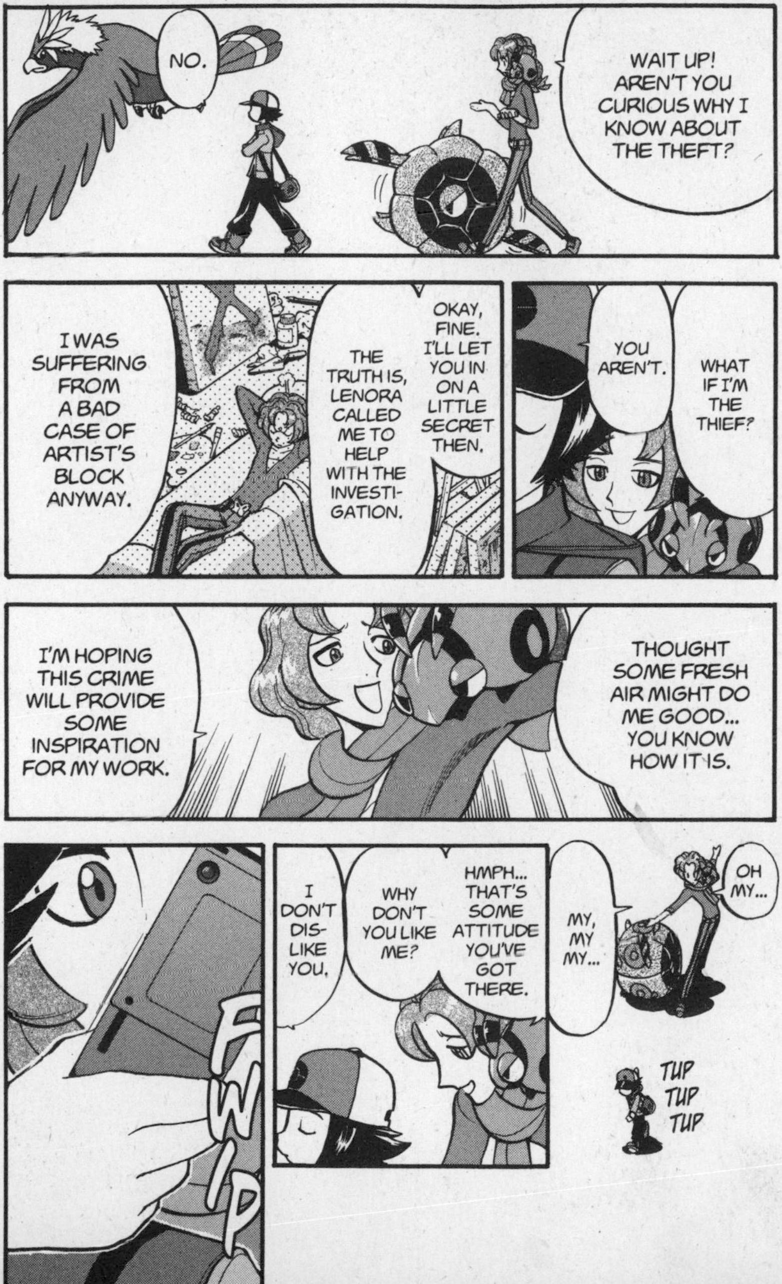
WAIT UP! AREN'T YOU CURIOUS WHY I KNOW ABOUT THE THEFT?
NO.
WHAT IF I'M THE THIEF?
YOU AREN'T.
OKAY, FINE. I'LL LET YOU IN ON A LITTLE SECRET THEN.
THE TRUTH IS, LENORA CALLED ME TO HELP WITH THE INVESTI-GATION.
I WAS SUFFERING FROM A BAD CASE OF ARTIST'S BLOCK ANYWAY.
THOUGHT SOME FRESH AIR MIGHT DO ME GOOD... YOU KNOW HOW IT IS.
I'M HOPING THIS CRIME WILL PROVIDE SOME INSPIRATION FOR MY WORK.
OH MY...
MY, MY MY...
TUP TUP TUP
HMPH... THAT'S SOME ATTITUDE YOU'VE GOT THERE.
WHY DON'T YOU LIKE ME?
I DON'T DIS-LIKE YOU.
FWIP

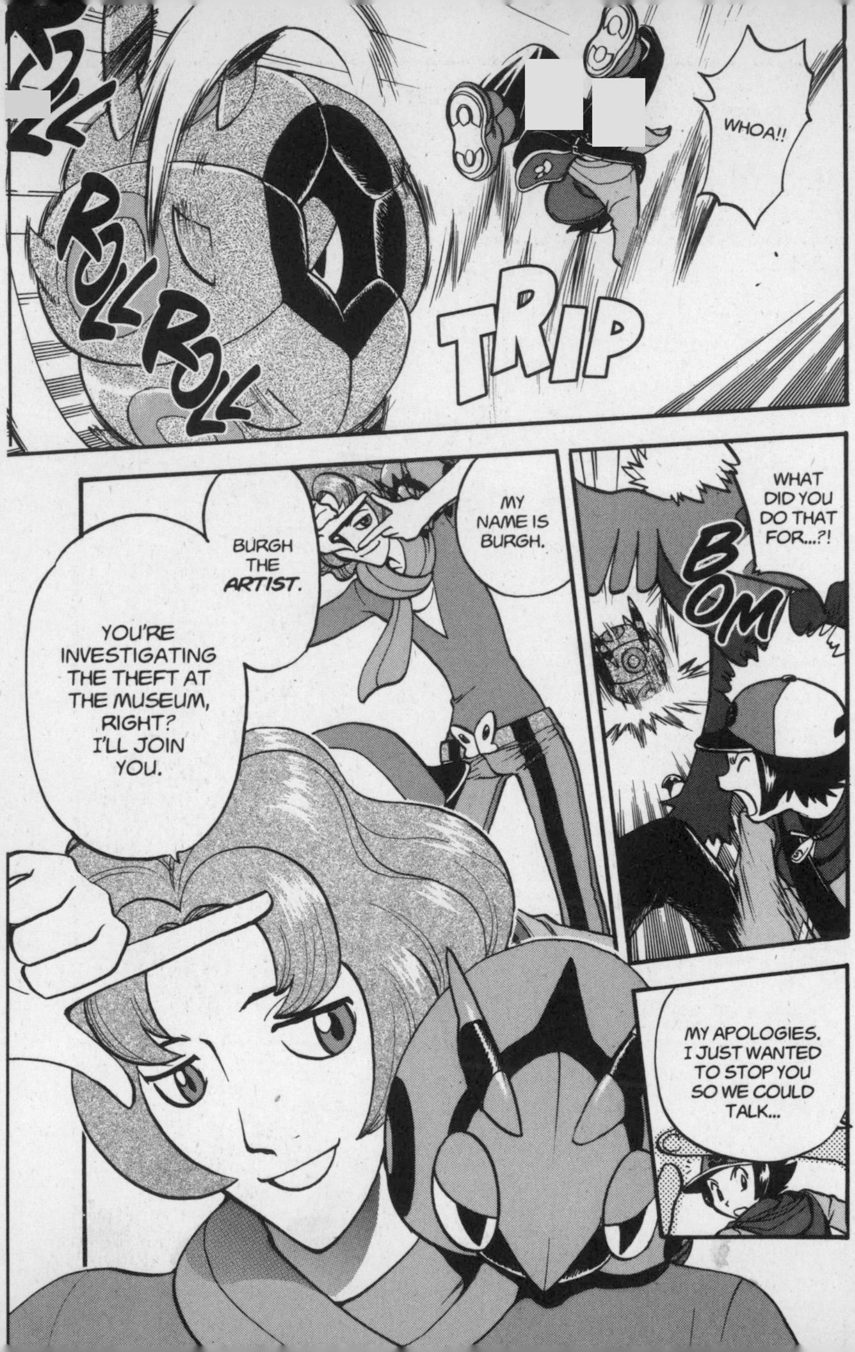
WHOA!!
TRIP
ROLL ROLL
WHAT DID YOU DO THAT FOR...?!
BOM
MY APOLOGIES. I JUST WANTED TO STOP YOU SO WE COULD TALK...
MY NAME IS BURGH.
BURGH THE ARTIST.
YOU'RE INVESTIGATING THE THEFT AT THE MUSEUM, RIGHT? I'LL JOIN YOU.

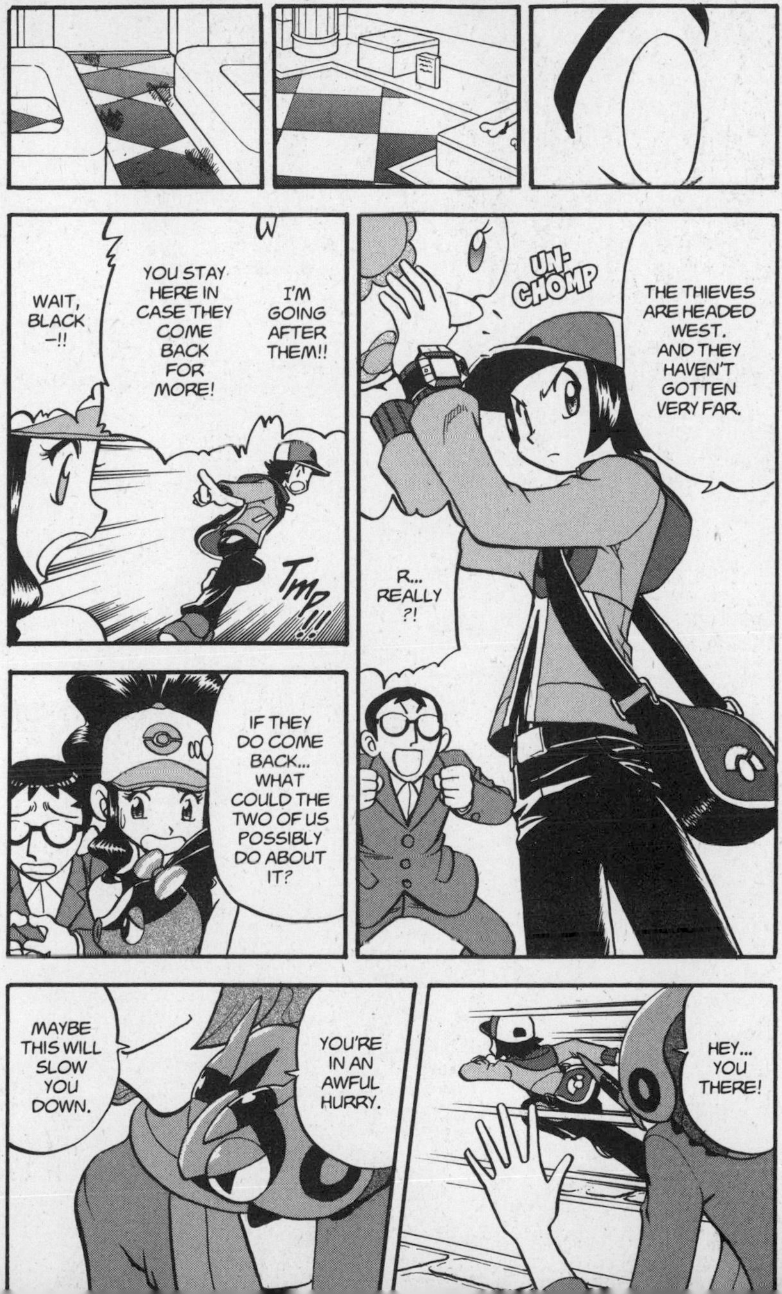
UN-CHOMP
THE THIEVES ARE HEADED WEST. AND THEY HAVEN'T GOTTEN VERY FAR.
R... REALLY?!
I'M GOING AFTER THEM!!
YOU STAY HERE IN CASE THEY COME BACK FOR MORE!
WAIT, BLACK—!!
TMP!!
IF THEY DO COME BACK... WHAT COULD THE TWO OF US POSSIBLY DO ABOUT IT?
HEY... YOU THERE!
YOU'RE IN AN AWFUL HURRY.
MAYBE THIS WILL SLOW YOU DOWN.

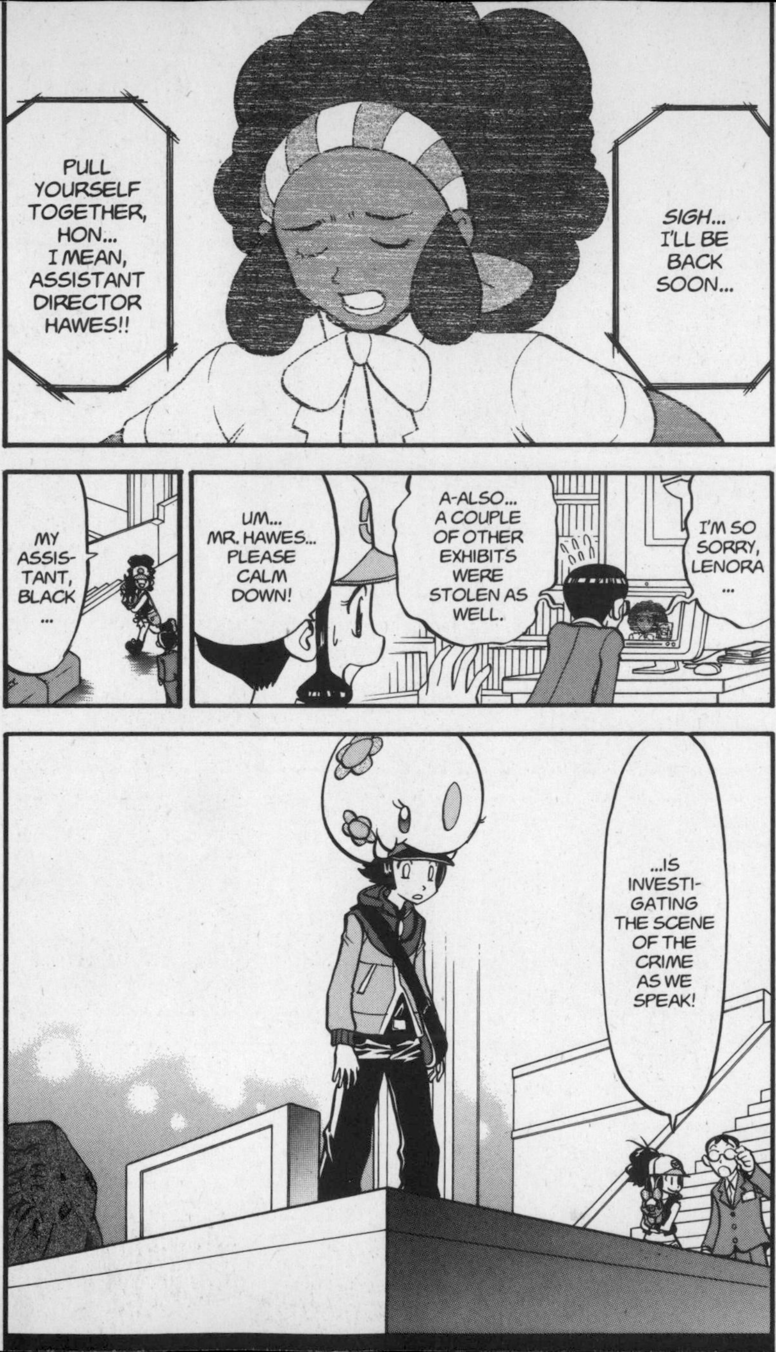
SIGH... I'LL BE BACK SOON...
PULL YOURSELF TOGETHER, HON... I MEAN, ASSISTANT DIRECTOR HAWES!!
I'M SO SORRY, LENORA ...
A-ALSO... A COUPLE OF OTHER EXHIBITS WERE STOLEN AS WELL.
UM... MR. HAWES... PLEASE CALM DOWN!
MY ASSIS-TANT, BLACK ...
...IS INVESTI-GATING THE SCENE OF THE CRIME AS WE SPEAK!

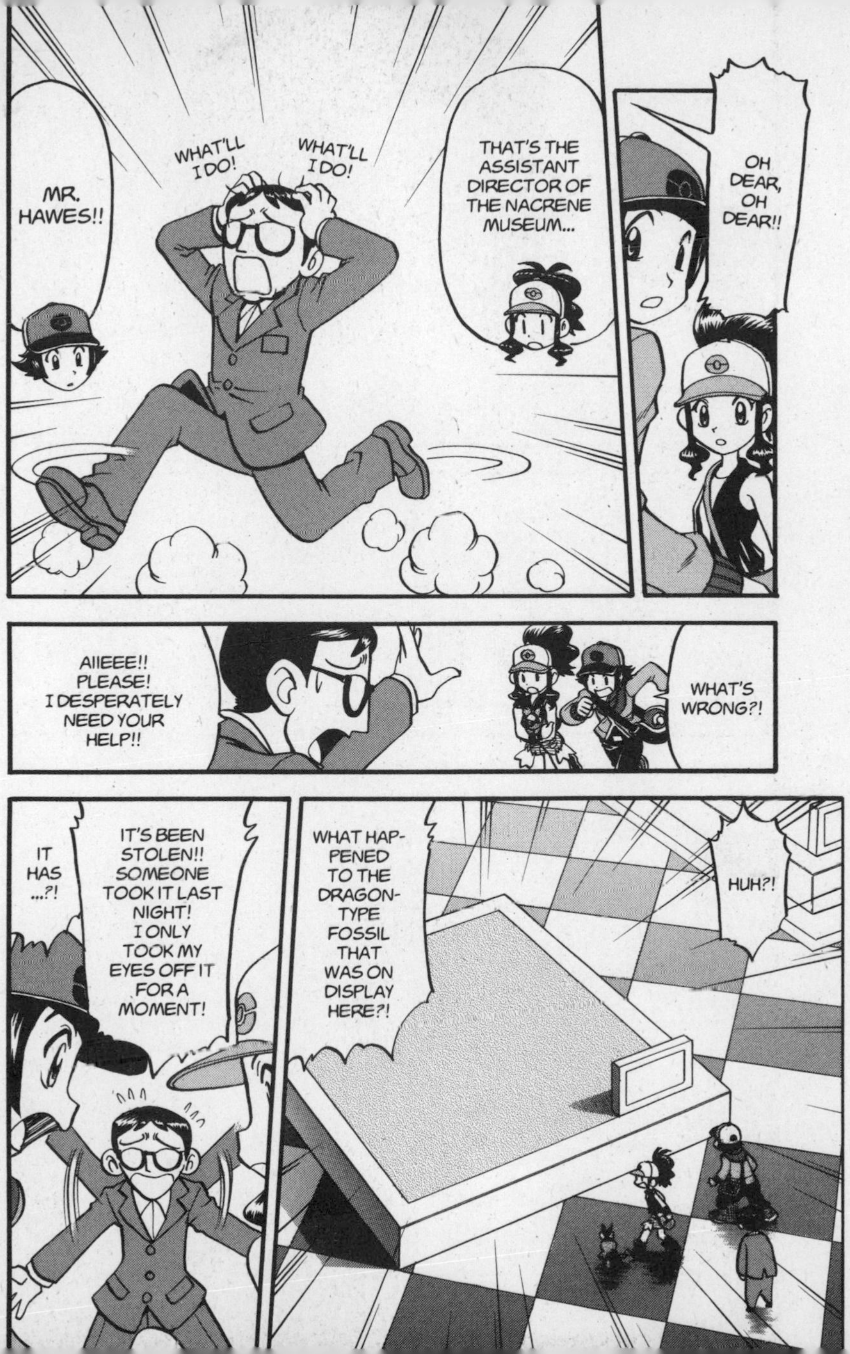
OH DEAR, OH DEAR!!
THAT'S THE ASSISTANT DIRECTOR OF THE NACRENE MUSEUM...
WHAT'LL I DO!
WHAT'LL I DO!
MR. HAWES!!
WHAT'S WRONG?!
AIIEEE!! PLEASE! I DESPERATELY NEED YOUR HELP!!
HUH?!
WHAT HAP-PENED TO THE DRAGON-TYPE FOSSIL THAT WAS ON DISPLAY HERE?!
IT'S BEEN STOLEN!! SOMEONE TOOK IT LAST NIGHT! I ONLY TOOK MY EYES OFF IT FOR A MOMENT!
IT HAS ...?!

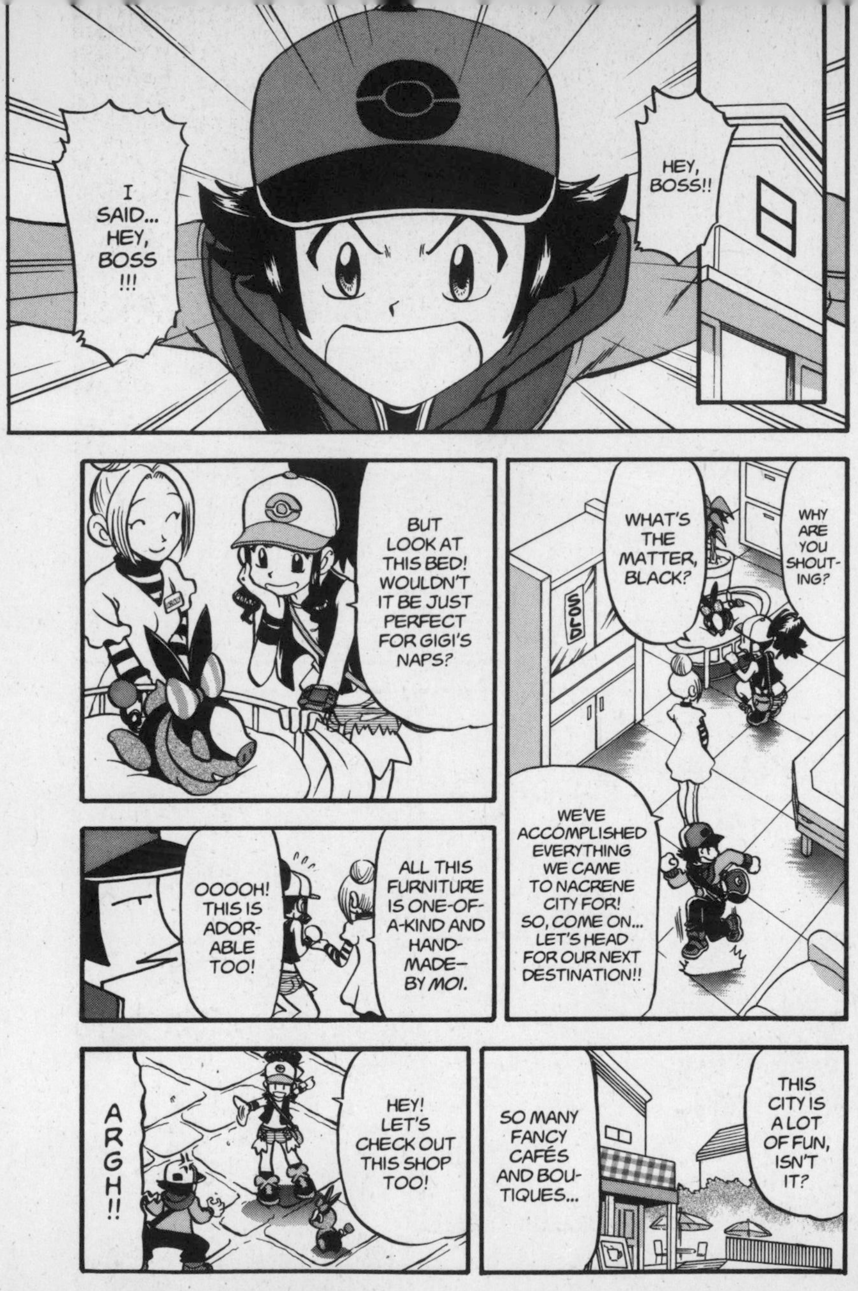
HEY, BOSS!!
I SAID... HEY, BOSS!!!
WHY ARE YOU SHOUT-ING?
WHAT'S THE MATTER, BLACK?
WE'VE ACCOMPLISHED EVERYTHING WE CAME TO NACRENE CITY FOR! SO, COME ON... LET'S HEAD FOR OUR NEXT DESTINATION!!
BUT LOOK AT THIS BED! WOULDN'T IT BE JUST PERFECT FOR GIGI'S NAPS?
SOLD
ALL THIS FURNITURE IS ONE-OF-A-KIND AND HAND-MADE—BY MOI.
OOOOH! THIS IS ADOR-ABLE TOO!
THIS CITY IS A LOT OF FUN, ISN'T IT?
SO MANY FANCY CAFÉS AND BOU-TIQUES...
HEY! LET'S CHECK OUT THIS SHOP TOO!
ARGH!!

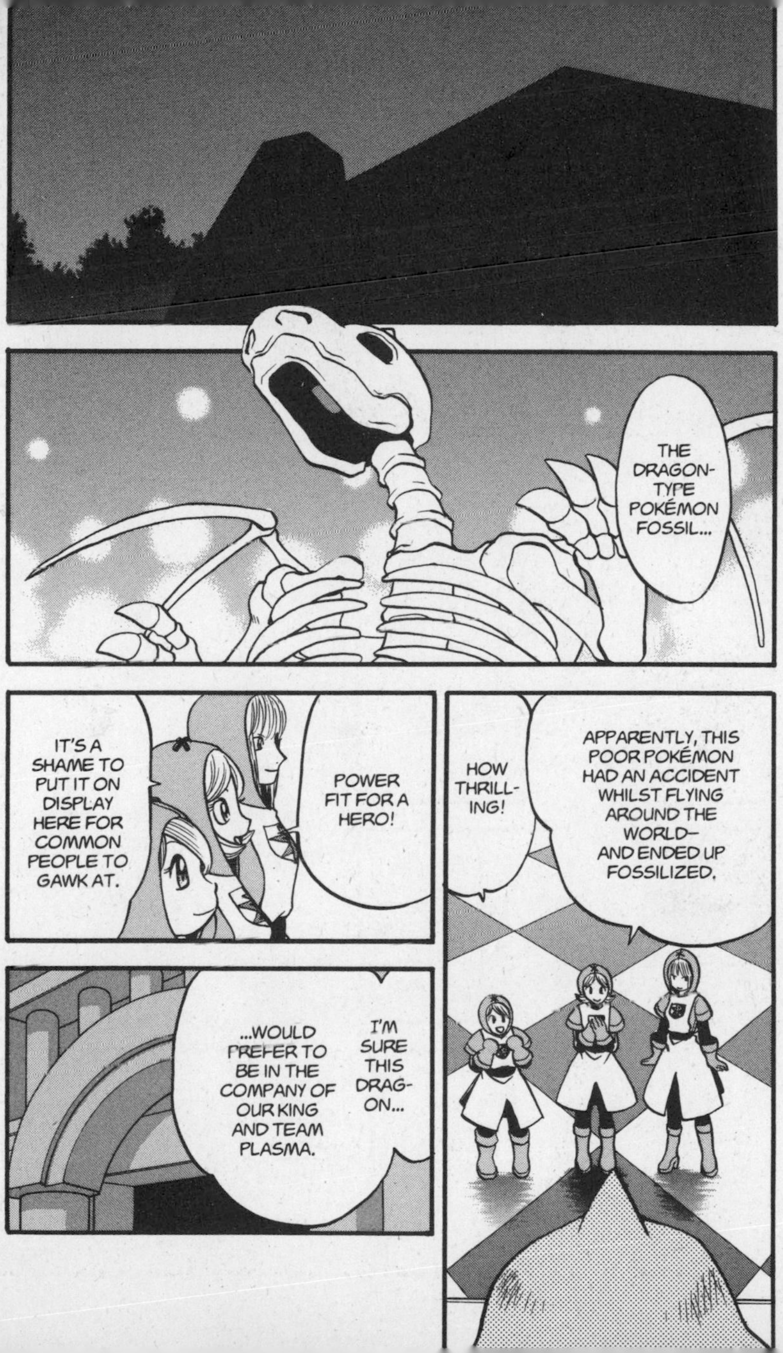
THE DRAGON-TYPE POKÉMON FOSSIL...
APPARENTLY, THIS POOR POKÉMON HAD AN ACCIDENT WHILST FLYING AROUND THE WORLD— AND ENDED UP FOSSILIZED.
HOW THRILL-ING!
POWER FIT FOR A HERO!
IT'S A SHAME TO PUT IT ON DISPLAY HERE FOR COMMON PEOPLE TO GAWK AT.
I'M SURE THIS DRAG-ON...
...WOULD PREFER TO BE IN THE COMPANY OF OUR KING AND TEAM PLASMA.

Adventure ⑮
The Mystery of the Missing Fossil

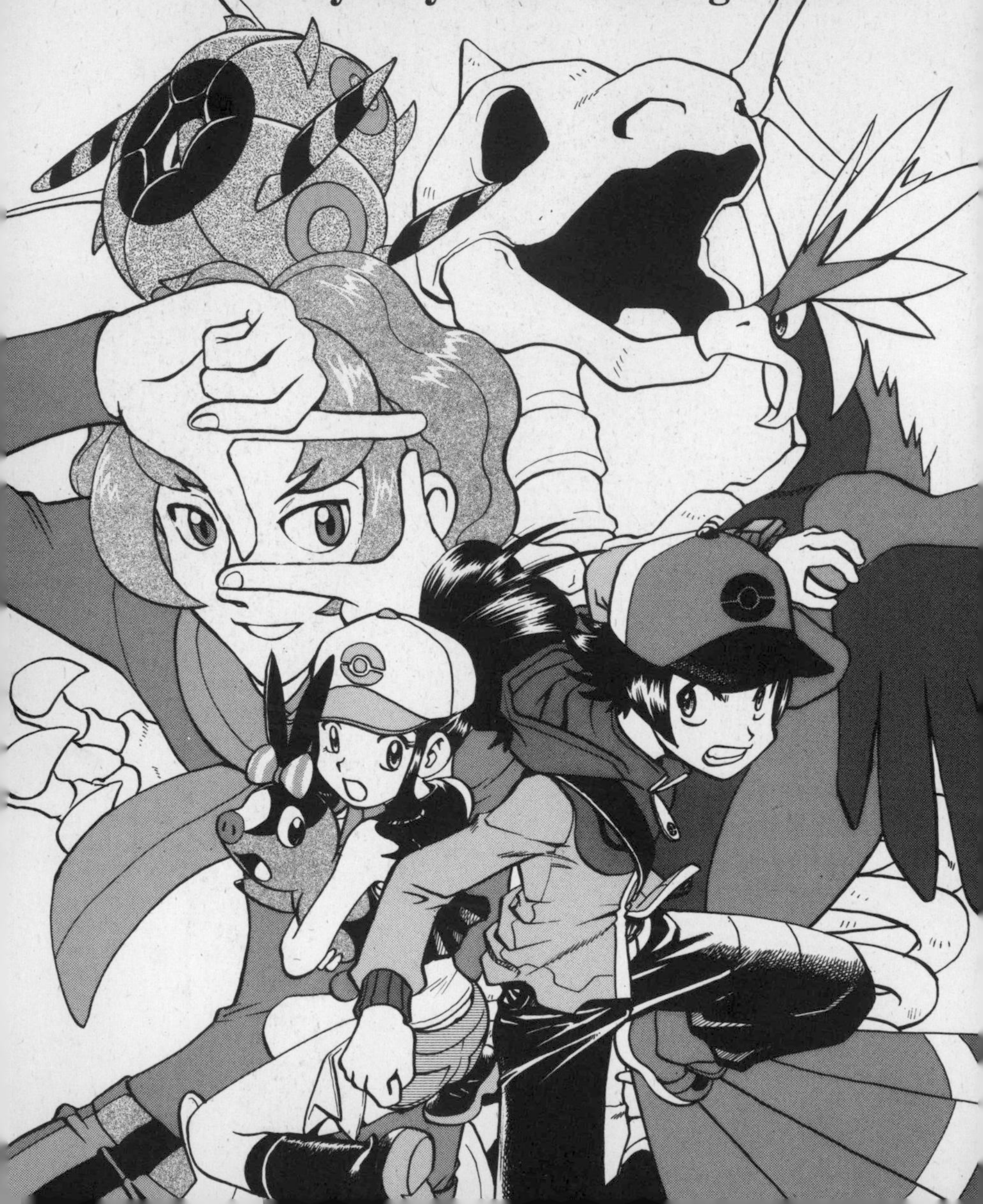

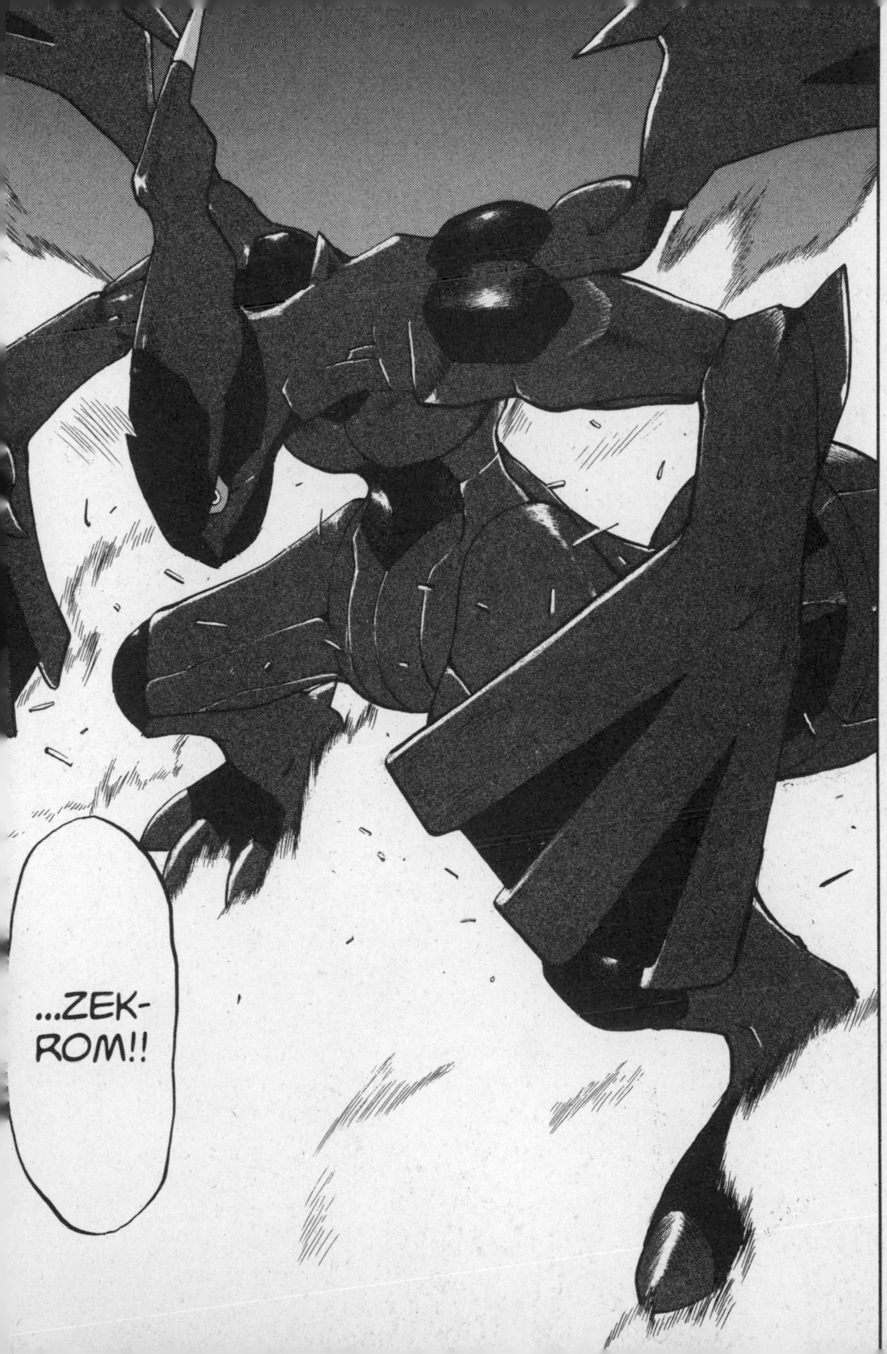
...ZEK-
ROM!!

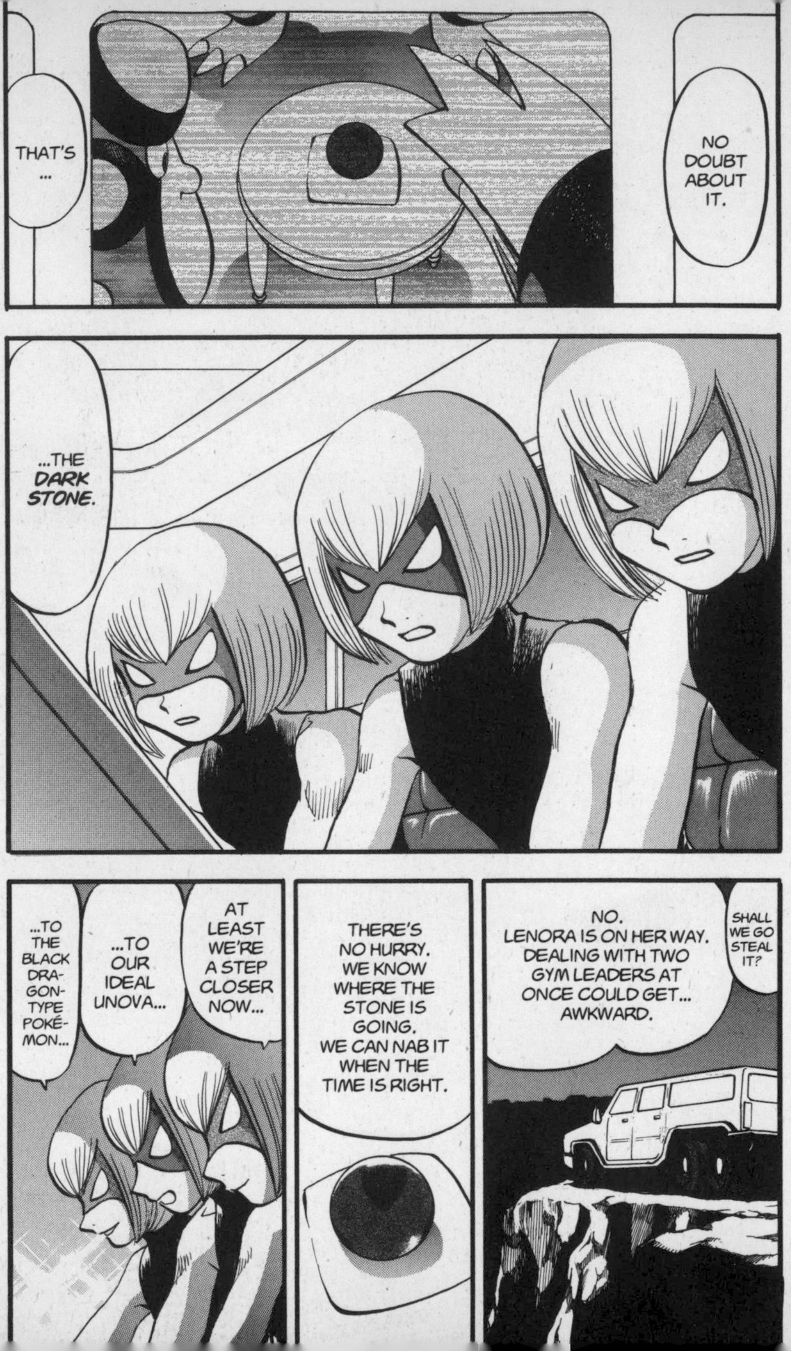
NO DOUBT ABOUT IT.
THAT'S ...
...THE *DARK STONE*.
SHALL WE GO STEAL IT?
NO. LENORA IS ON HER WAY. DEALING WITH TWO GYM LEADERS AT ONCE COULD GET... AWKWARD.
THERE'S NO HURRY. WE KNOW WHERE THE STONE IS GOING. WE CAN NAB IT WHEN THE TIME IS RIGHT.
AT LEAST WE'RE A STEP CLOSER NOW...
...TO OUR IDEAL UNOVA...
...TO THE BLACK DRA-GON-TYPE POKÉ-MON...

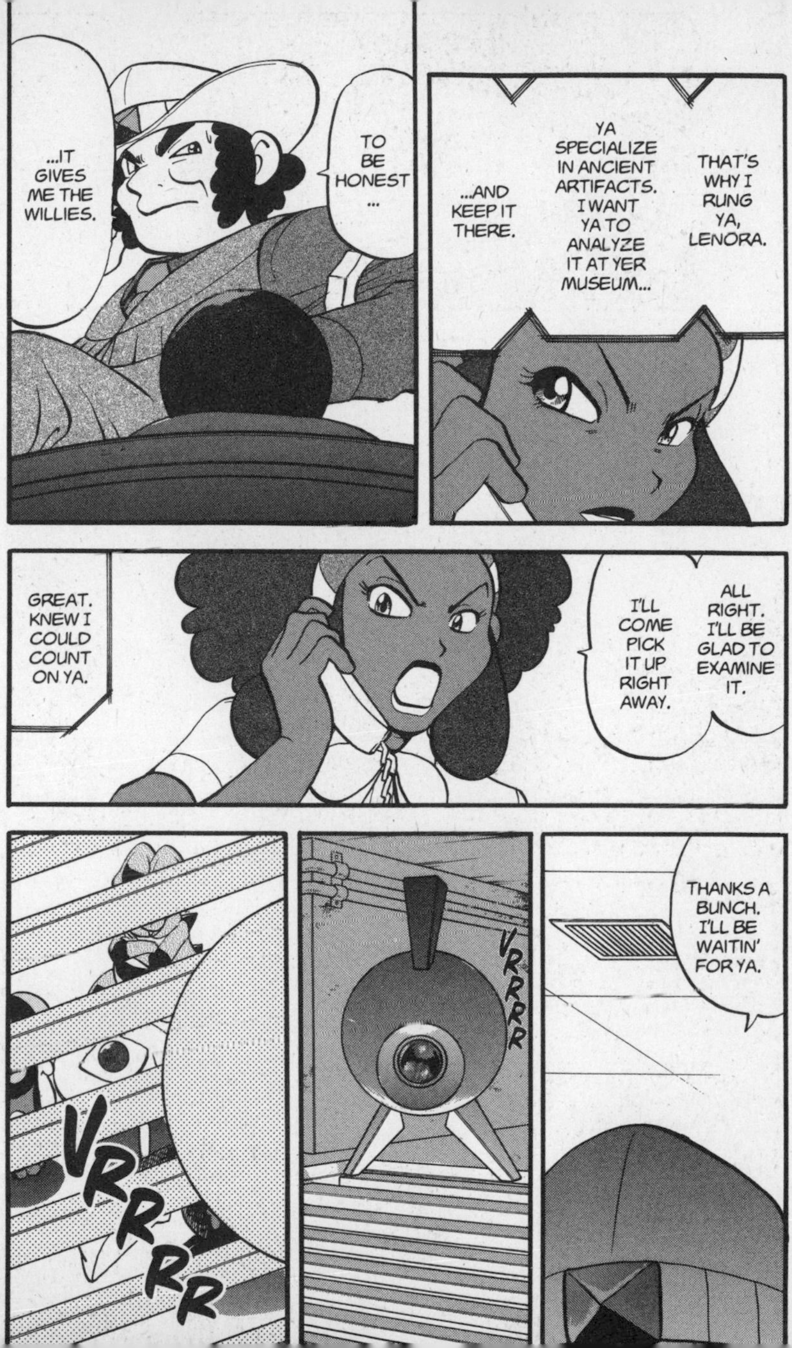
THAT'S WHY I RUNG YA, LENORA.
YA SPECIALIZE IN ANCIENT ARTIFACTS. I WANT YA TO ANALYZE IT AT YER MUSEUM...
...AND KEEP IT THERE.
TO BE HONEST ...
...IT GIVES ME THE WILLIES.
ALL RIGHT. I'LL BE GLAD TO EXAMINE IT.
I'LL COME PICK IT UP RIGHT AWAY.
GREAT. KNEW I COULD COUNT ON YA.
THANKS A BUNCH. I'LL BE WAITIN' FOR YA.
VRRRRR
VRRRRR

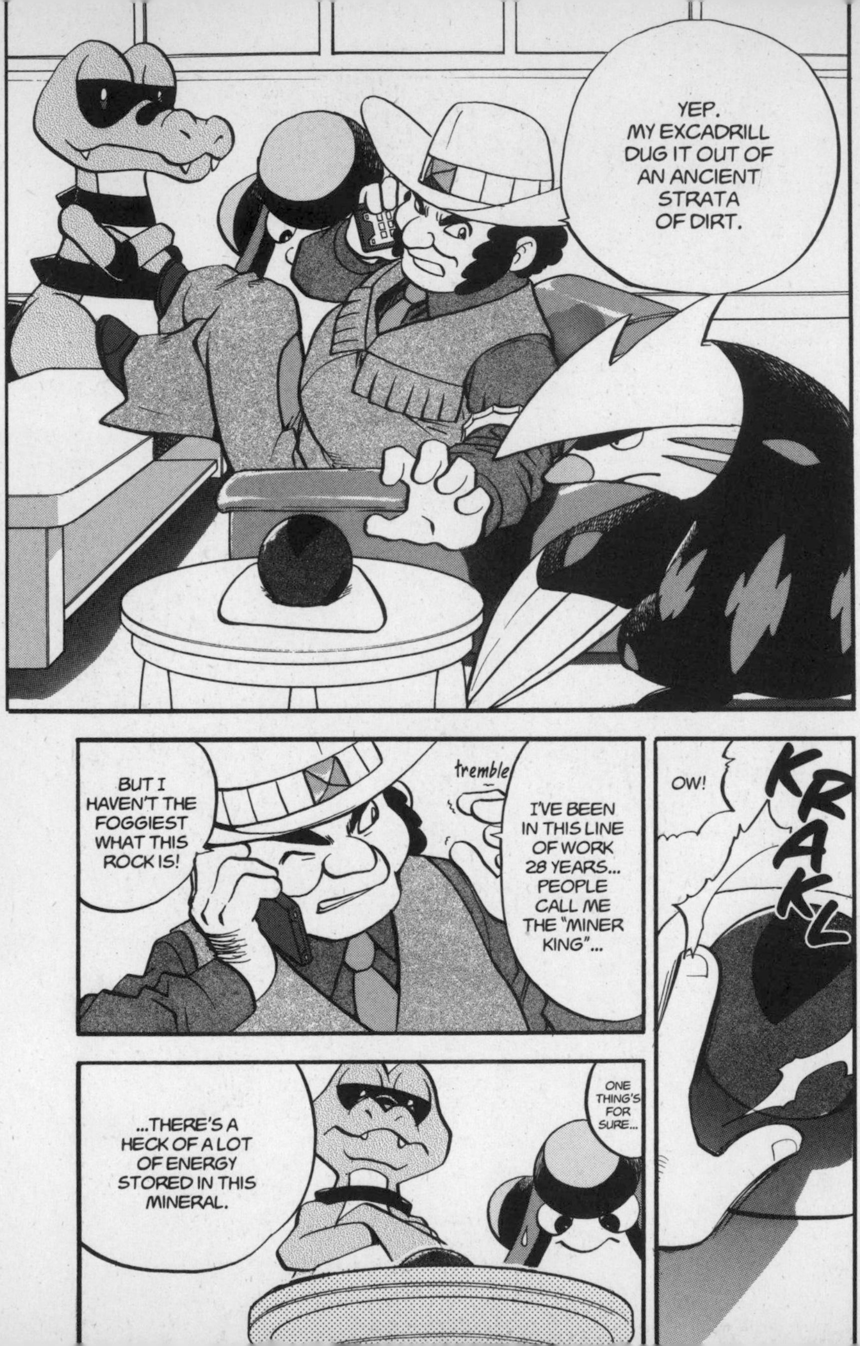
YEP. MY EXCADRILL DUG IT OUT OF AN ANCIENT STRATA OF DIRT.
BUT I HAVEN'T THE FOGGIEST WHAT THIS ROCK IS!
tremble
I'VE BEEN IN THIS LINE OF WORK 28 YEARS... PEOPLE CALL ME THE "MINER KING"...
KRAKL
OW!
ONE THING'S FOR SURE...
...THERE'S A HECK OF A LOT OF ENERGY STORED IN THIS MINERAL.

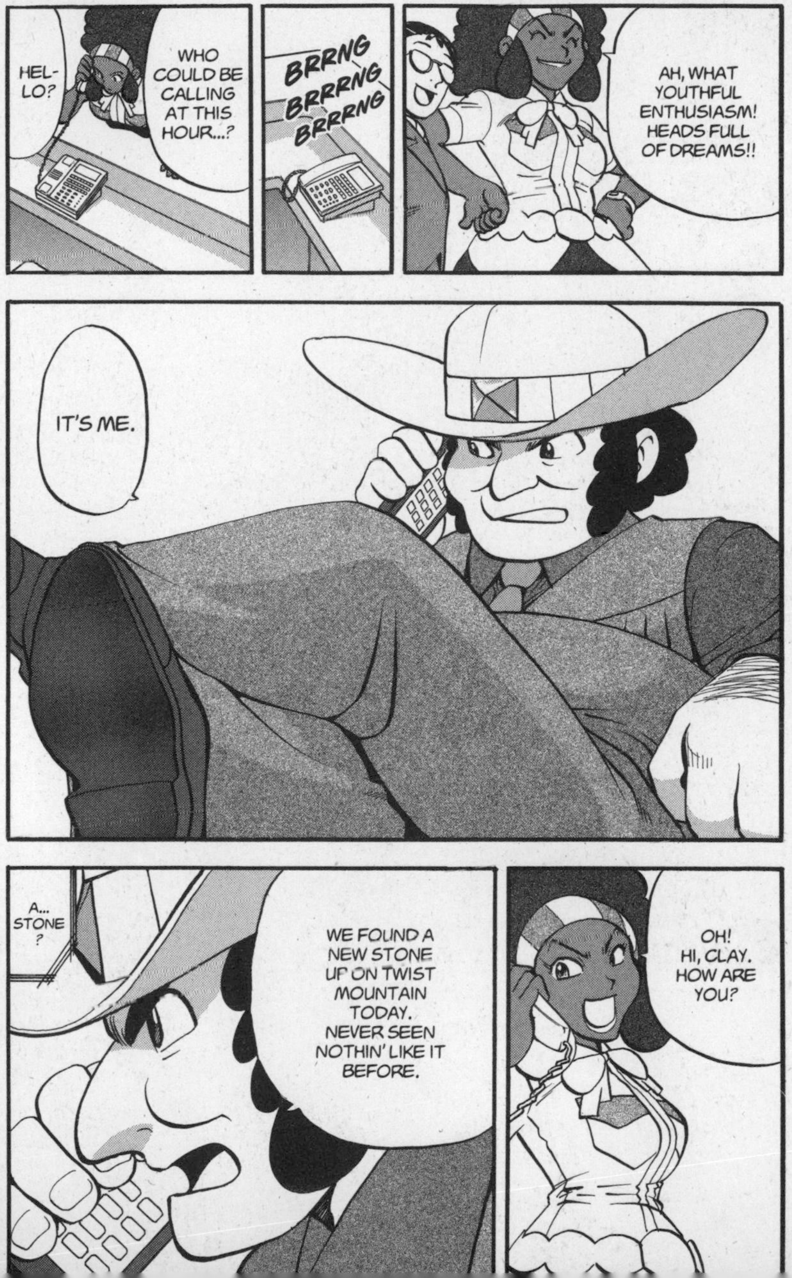
AH, WHAT YOUTHFUL ENTHUSIASM! HEADS FULL OF DREAMS!!
BRRNG
BRRRNG
BRRRNG
WHO COULD BE CALLING AT THIS HOUR...?
HEL-LO?
IT'S ME.
OH! HI, CLAY. HOW ARE YOU?
WE FOUND A NEW STONE UP ON TWIST MOUNTAIN TODAY. NEVER SEEN NOTHIN' LIKE IT BEFORE.
A... STONE?

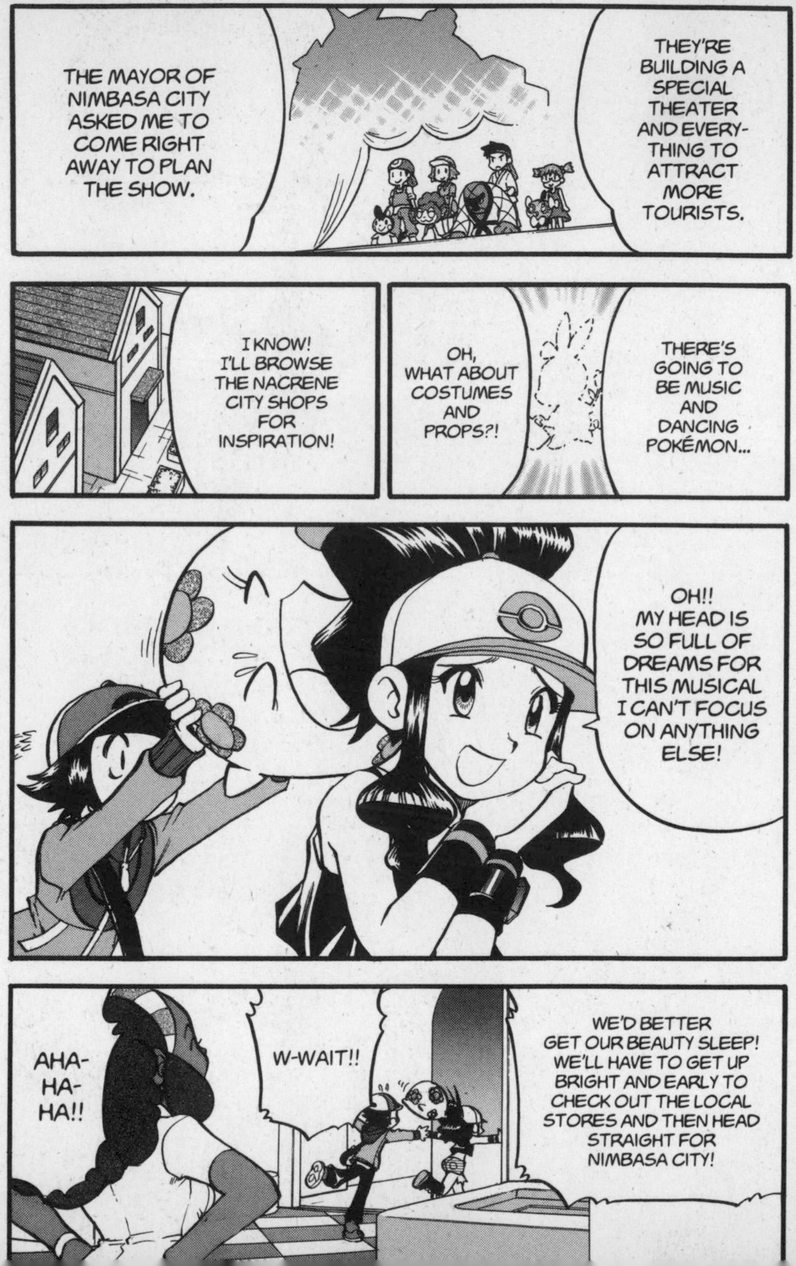

THE MAYOR OF NIMBASA CITY ASKED ME TO COME RIGHT AWAY TO PLAN THE SHOW.
THEY'RE BUILDING A SPECIAL THEATER AND EVERY-THING TO ATTRACT MORE TOURISTS.
I KNOW! I'LL BROWSE THE NACRENE CITY SHOPS FOR INSPIRATION!
OH, WHAT ABOUT COSTUMES AND PROPS?!
THERE'S GOING TO BE MUSIC AND DANCING POKÉMON...
OH!! MY HEAD IS SO FULL OF DREAMS FOR THIS MUSICAL I CAN'T FOCUS ON ANYTHING ELSE!
AHA-HA-HA!!
W-WAIT!!
WE'D BETTER GET OUR BEAUTY SLEEP! WE'LL HAVE TO GET UP BRIGHT AND EARLY TO CHECK OUT THE LOCAL STORES AND THEN HEAD STRAIGHT FOR NIMBASA CITY!

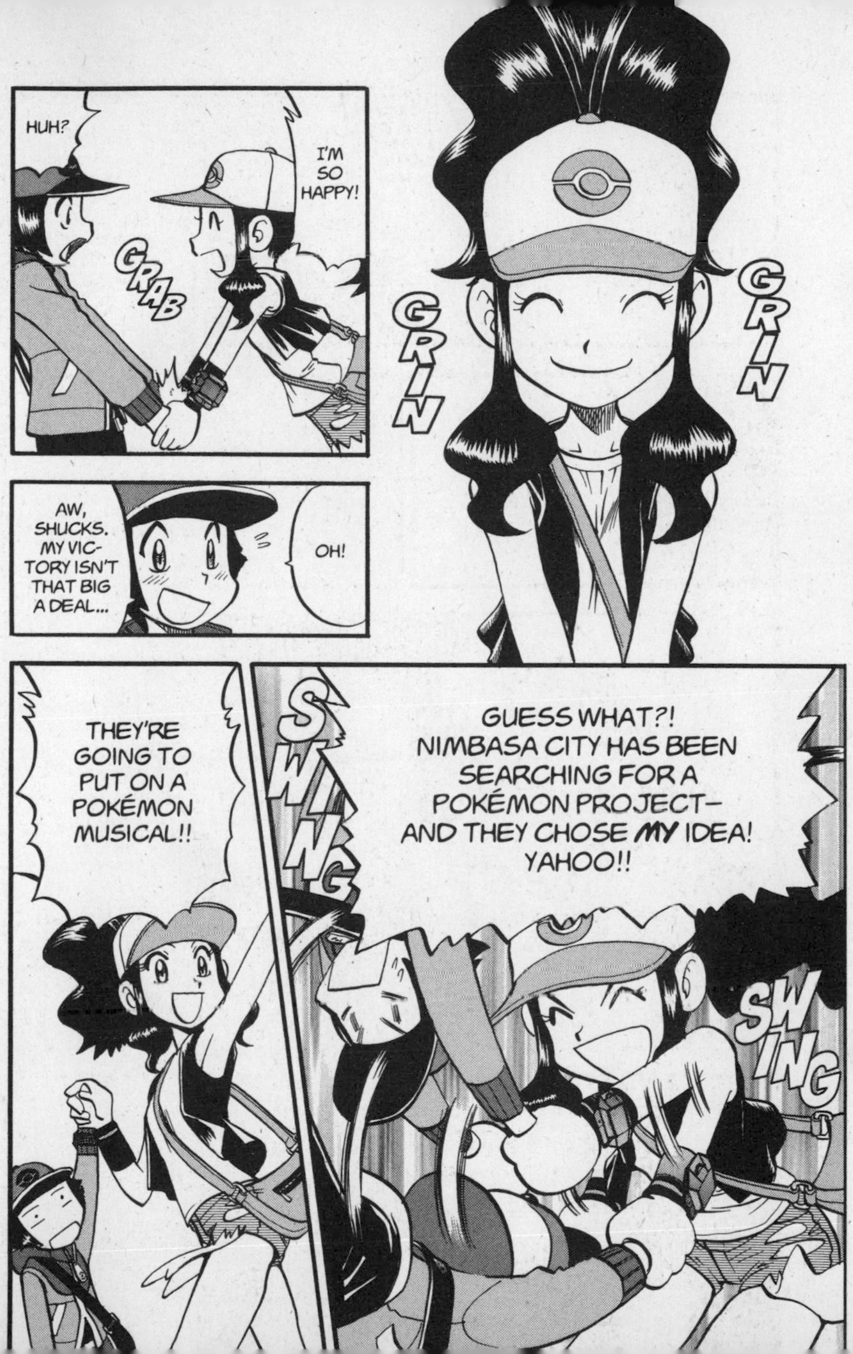
HUH?
I'M SO HAPPY!
GRAB
AW, SHUCKS. MY VICTORY ISN'T THAT BIG A DEAL...
OH!
GRIN
GRIN
THEY'RE GOING TO PUT ON A POKÉMON MUSICAL!!
SWING
GUESS WHAT?! NIMBASA CITY HAS BEEN SEARCHING FOR A POKÉMON PROJECT—AND THEY CHOSE MY IDEA! YAHOO!!
SWING

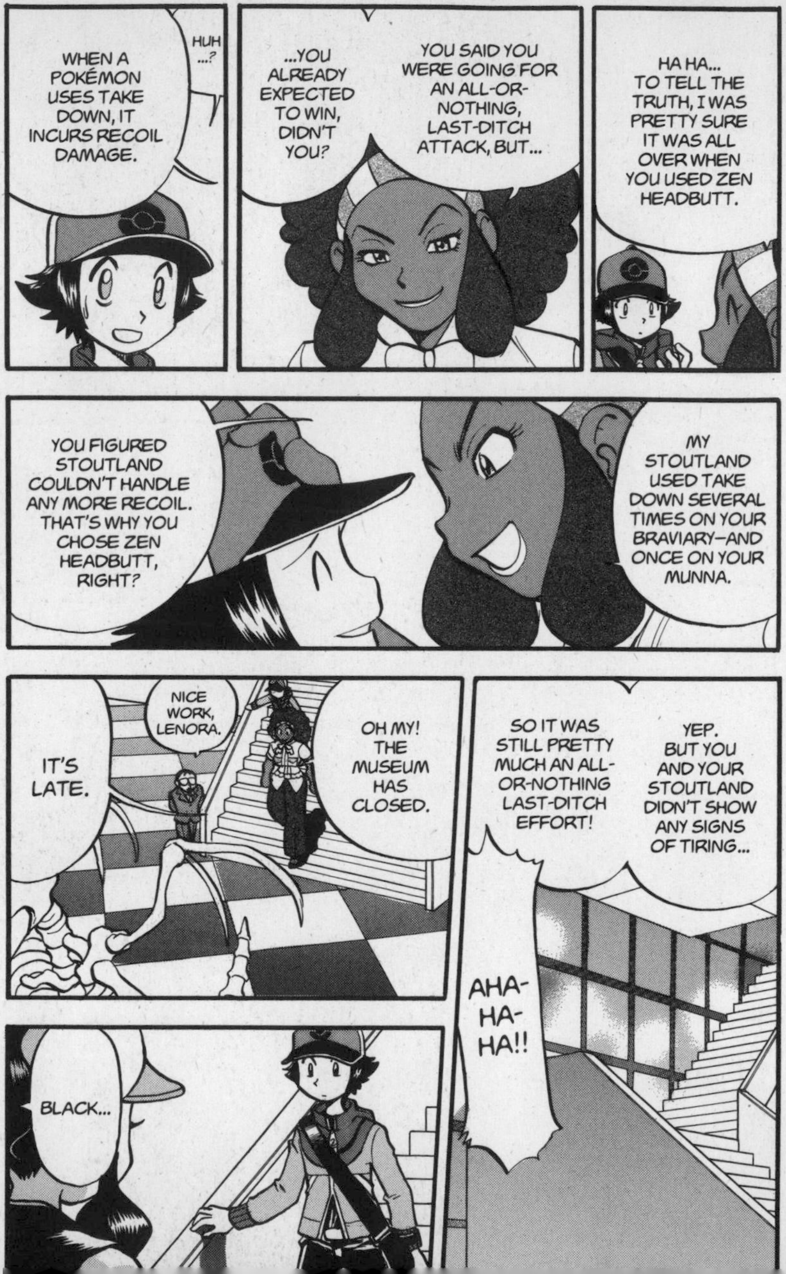
HA HA... TO TELL THE TRUTH, I WAS PRETTY SURE IT WAS ALL OVER WHEN YOU USED ZEN HEADBUTT.
YOU SAID YOU WERE GOING FOR AN ALL-OR-NOTHING, LAST-DITCH ATTACK, BUT...
...YOU ALREADY EXPECTED TO WIN, DIDN'T YOU?
HUH ...?
WHEN A POKÉMON USES TAKE DOWN, IT INCURS RECOIL DAMAGE.
MY STOUTLAND USED TAKE DOWN SEVERAL TIMES ON YOUR BRAVIARY—AND ONCE ON YOUR MUNNA.
YOU FIGURED STOUTLAND COULDN'T HANDLE ANY MORE RECOIL. THAT'S WHY YOU CHOSE ZEN HEADBUTT, RIGHT?
YEP. BUT YOU AND YOUR STOUTLAND DIDN'T SHOW ANY SIGNS OF TIRING...
SO IT WAS STILL PRETTY MUCH AN ALL-OR-NOTHING LAST-DITCH EFFORT!
AHA-HA-HA!!
OH MY! THE MUSEUM HAS CLOSED.
NICE WORK, LENORA.
IT'S LATE.
BLACK...

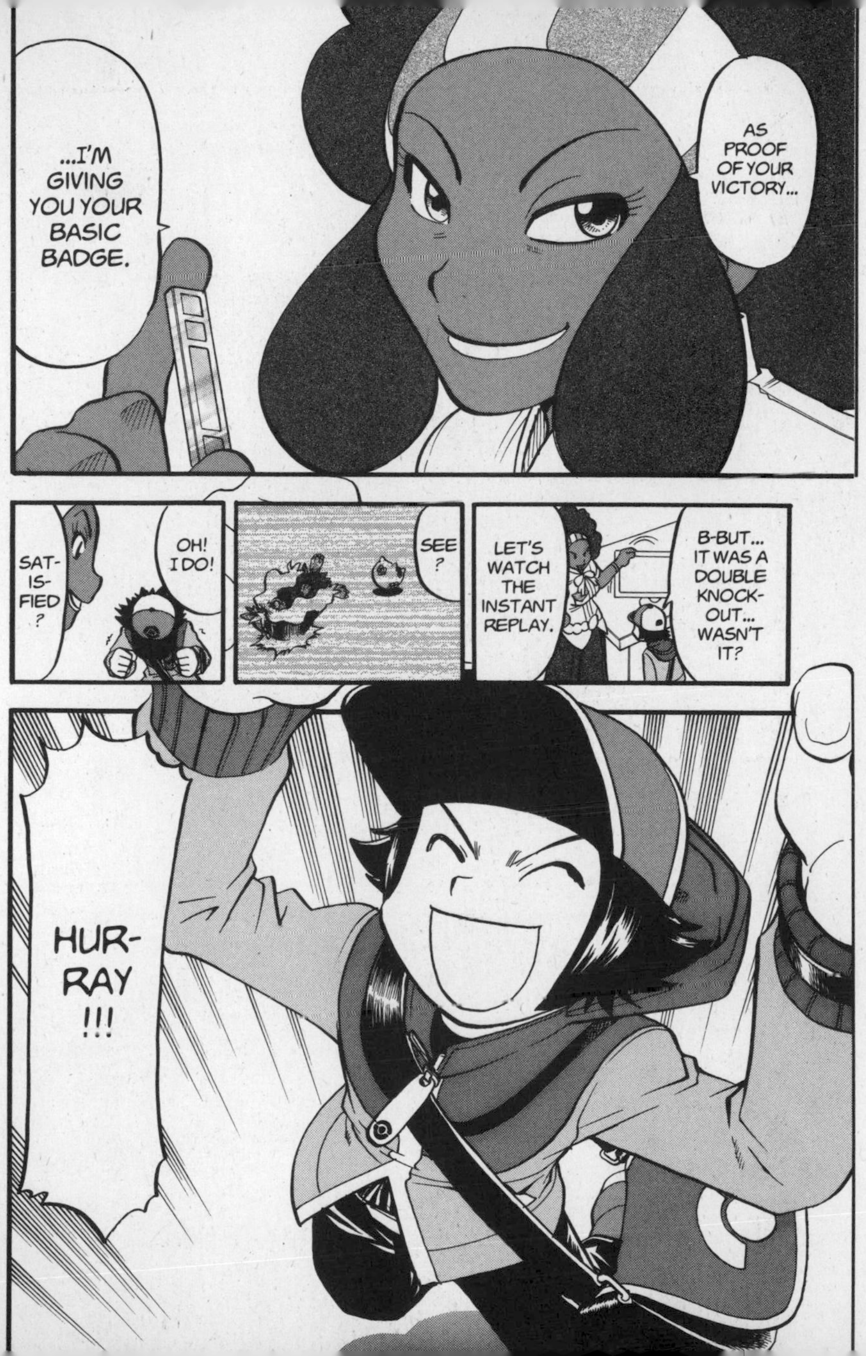
AS PROOF OF YOUR VICTORY...
...I'M GIVING YOU YOUR BASIC BADGE.
B-BUT... IT WAS A DOUBLE KNOCK-OUT... WASN'T IT?
LET'S WATCH THE INSTANT REPLAY.
SEE?
OH! I DO!
SAT-IS-FIED?
HUR-RAY!!!

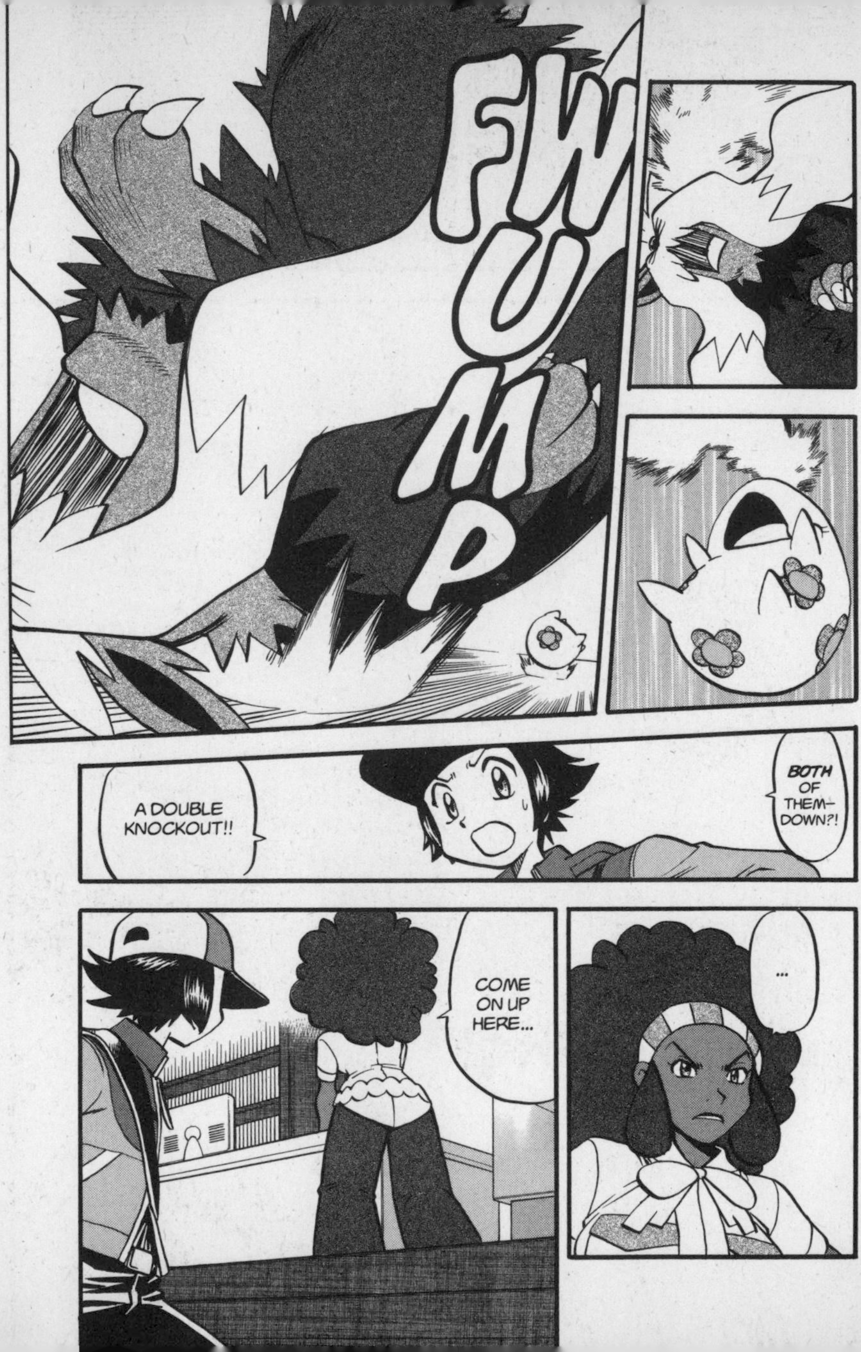
FWUMP
BOTH OF THEM— DOWN?!
A DOUBLE KNOCKOUT!!
...
COME ON UP HERE...

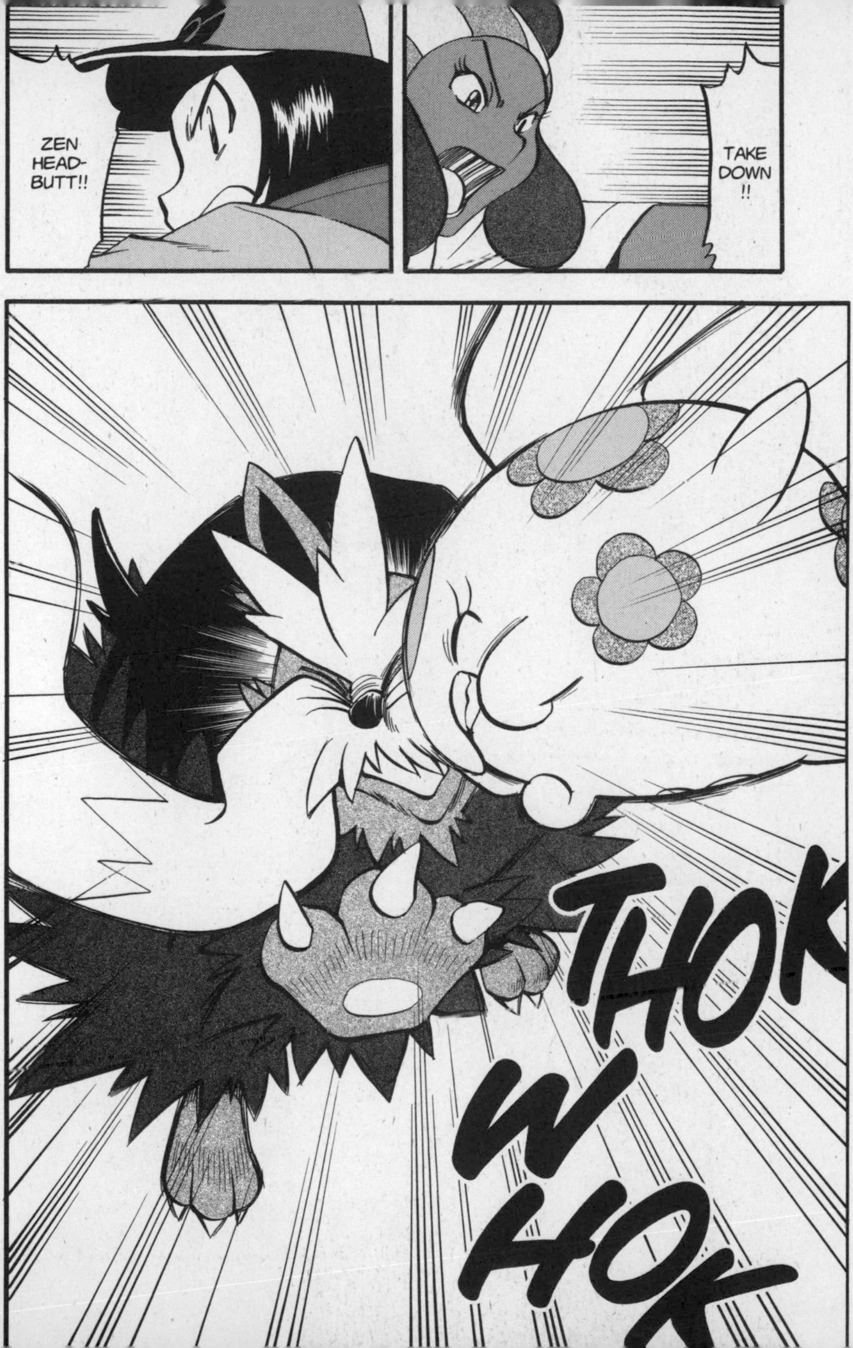
TAKE DOWN !!
ZEN HEAD-BUTT!!
THOK
W
HOK

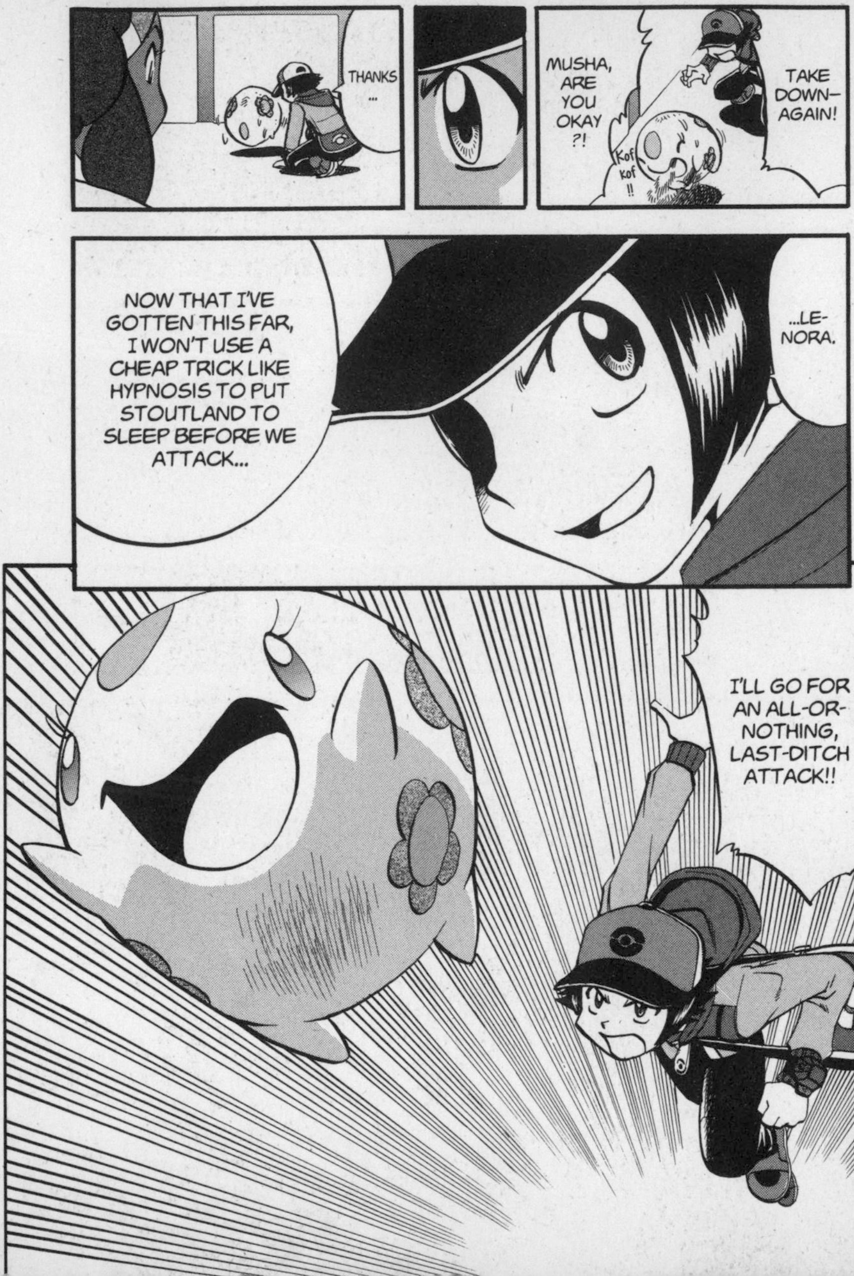
THANKS ...
MUSHA, ARE YOU OKAY ?!
Kof kof !!
TAKE DOWN—AGAIN!
...LE-NORA.
NOW THAT I'VE GOTTEN THIS FAR, I WON'T USE A CHEAP TRICK LIKE HYPNOSIS TO PUT STOUTLAND TO SLEEP BEFORE WE ATTACK...
I'LL GO FOR AN ALL-OR-NOTHING, LAST-DITCH ATTACK!!

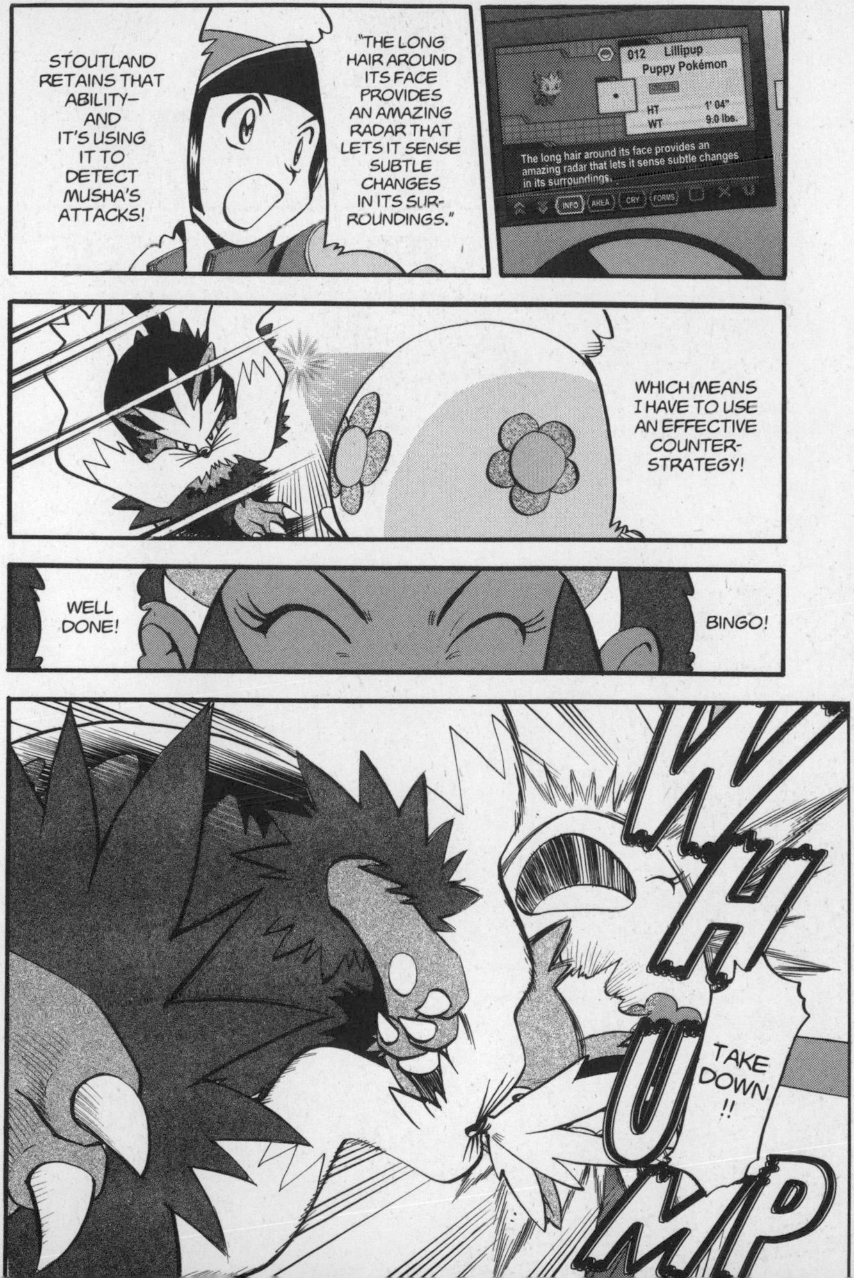
STOUTLAND RETAINS THAT ABILITY— AND IT'S USING IT TO DETECT MUSHA'S ATTACKS!
"THE LONG HAIR AROUND ITS FACE PROVIDES AN AMAZING RADAR THAT LETS IT SENSE SUBTLE CHANGES IN ITS SURROUNDINGS."
012 Lillipup
Puppy Pokémon
HT 1' 04"
WT 9.0 lbs.
The long hair around its face provides an amazing radar that lets it sense subtle changes in its surroundings.
INFO AREA CRY FORMS
WHICH MEANS I HAVE TO USE AN EFFECTIVE COUNTER-STRATEGY!
WELL DONE!
BINGO!
WHUMP
TAKE DOWN!!

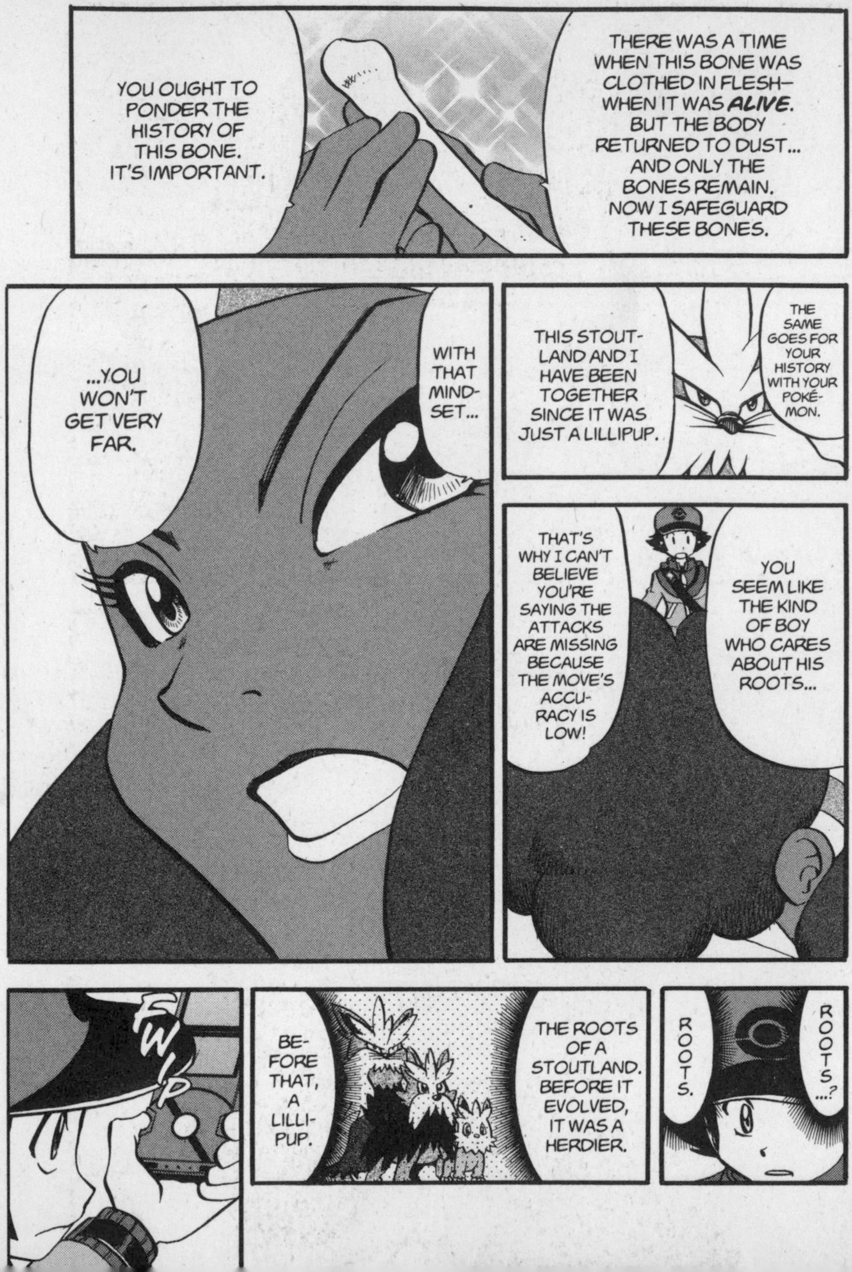
YOU OUGHT TO PONDER THE HISTORY OF THIS BONE. IT'S IMPORTANT.
THERE WAS A TIME WHEN THIS BONE WAS CLOTHED IN FLESH— WHEN IT WAS *ALIVE*. BUT THE BODY RETURNED TO DUST... AND ONLY THE BONES REMAIN. NOW I SAFEGUARD THESE BONES.
THIS STOUT-LAND AND I HAVE BEEN TOGETHER SINCE IT WAS JUST A LILLIPUP.
THE SAME GOES FOR YOUR HISTORY WITH YOUR POKÉ-MON.
YOU SEEM LIKE THE KIND OF BOY WHO CARES ABOUT HIS ROOTS...
THAT'S WHY I CAN'T BELIEVE YOU'RE SAYING THE ATTACKS ARE MISSING BECAUSE THE MOVE'S ACCU-RACY IS LOW!
WITH THAT MIND-SET...
...YOU WON'T GET VERY FAR.
ROOTS...?
ROOTS.
THE ROOTS OF A STOUTLAND. BEFORE IT EVOLVED, IT WAS A HERDIER.
BE-FORE THAT, A LILLI-PUP.
FWIP

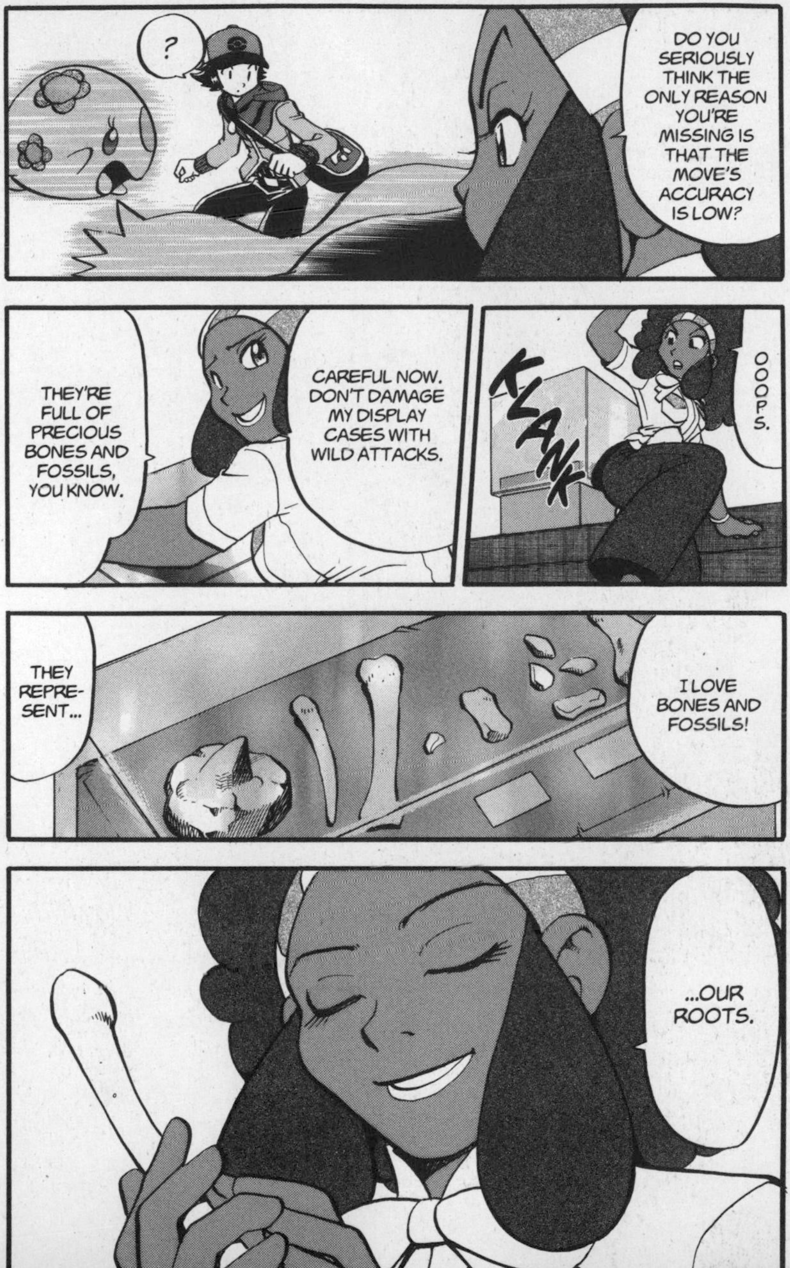
?
DO YOU SERIOUSLY THINK THE ONLY REASON YOU'RE MISSING IS THAT THE MOVE'S ACCURACY IS LOW?
OOOPS.
KLANK
CAREFUL NOW. DON'T DAMAGE MY DISPLAY CASES WITH WILD ATTACKS.
THEY'RE FULL OF PRECIOUS BONES AND FOSSILS, YOU KNOW.
I LOVE BONES AND FOSSILS!
THEY REPRESENT...
...OUR ROOTS.

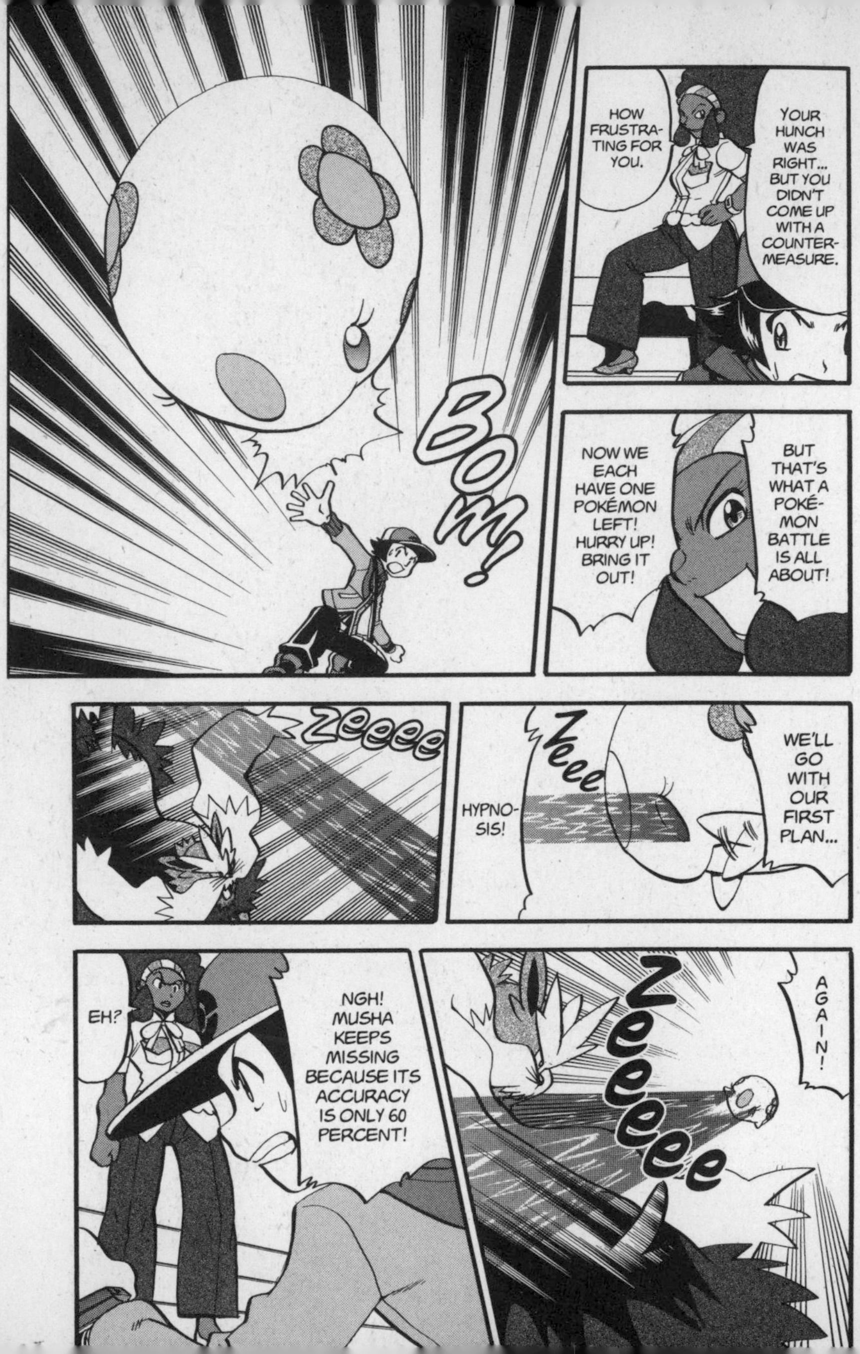

YOUR HUNCH WAS RIGHT... BUT YOU DIDN'T COME UP WITH A COUNTER-MEASURE.
HOW FRUSTRATING FOR YOU.
BUT THAT'S WHAT A POKÉ-MON BATTLE IS ALL ABOUT!
NOW WE EACH HAVE ONE POKÉMON LEFT! HURRY UP! BRING IT OUT!
BOOM!
WE'LL GO WITH OUR FIRST PLAN...
HYPNO-SIS!
Zeee
Zeeee
AGAIN!
Zeeeeee
NGH! MUSHA KEEPS MISSING BECAUSE ITS ACCURACY IS ONLY 60 PERCENT!
EH?

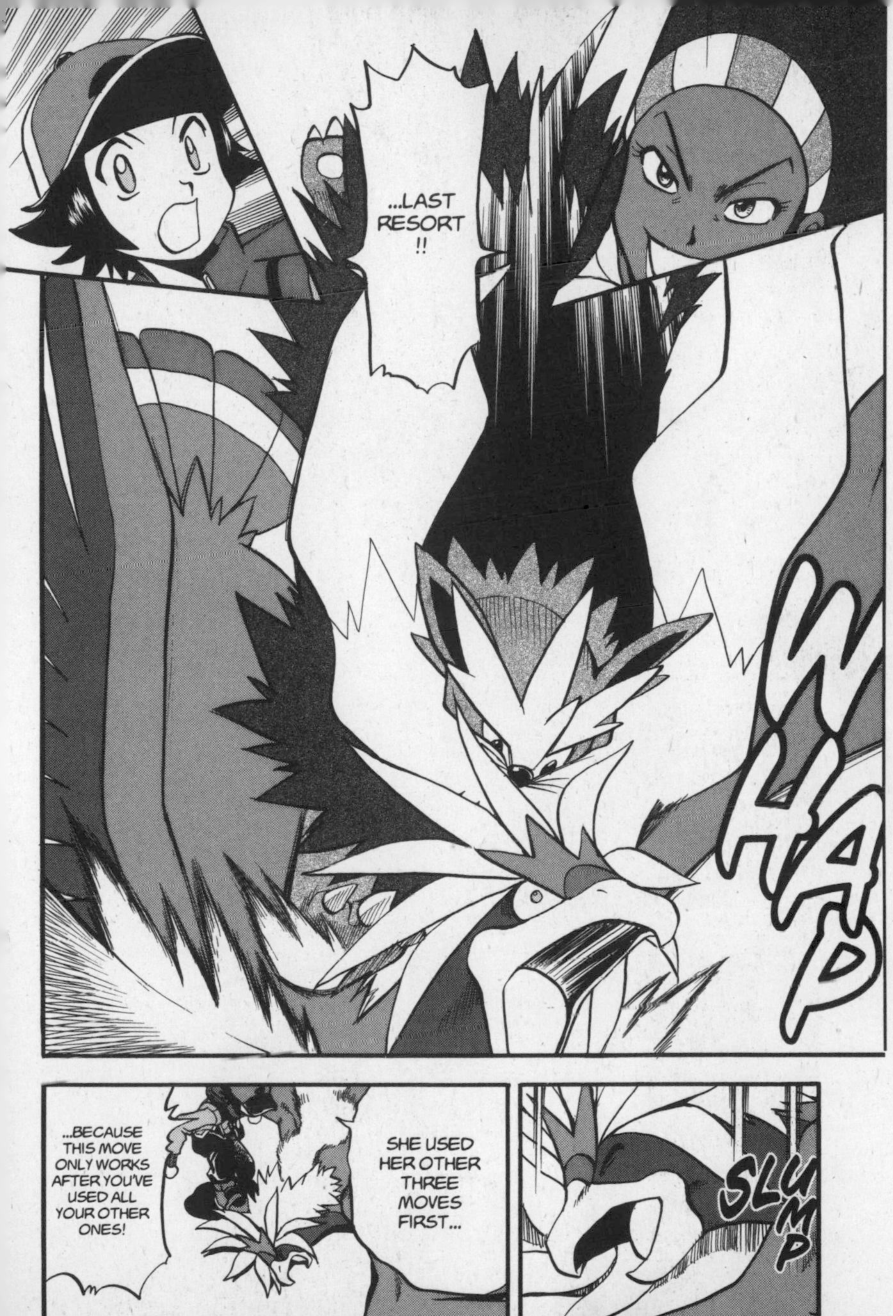
...LAST RESORT !!
WHAP
...BECAUSE THIS MOVE ONLY WORKS AFTER YOU'VE USED ALL YOUR OTHER ONES!
SHE USED HER OTHER THREE MOVES FIRST...
SLUMP

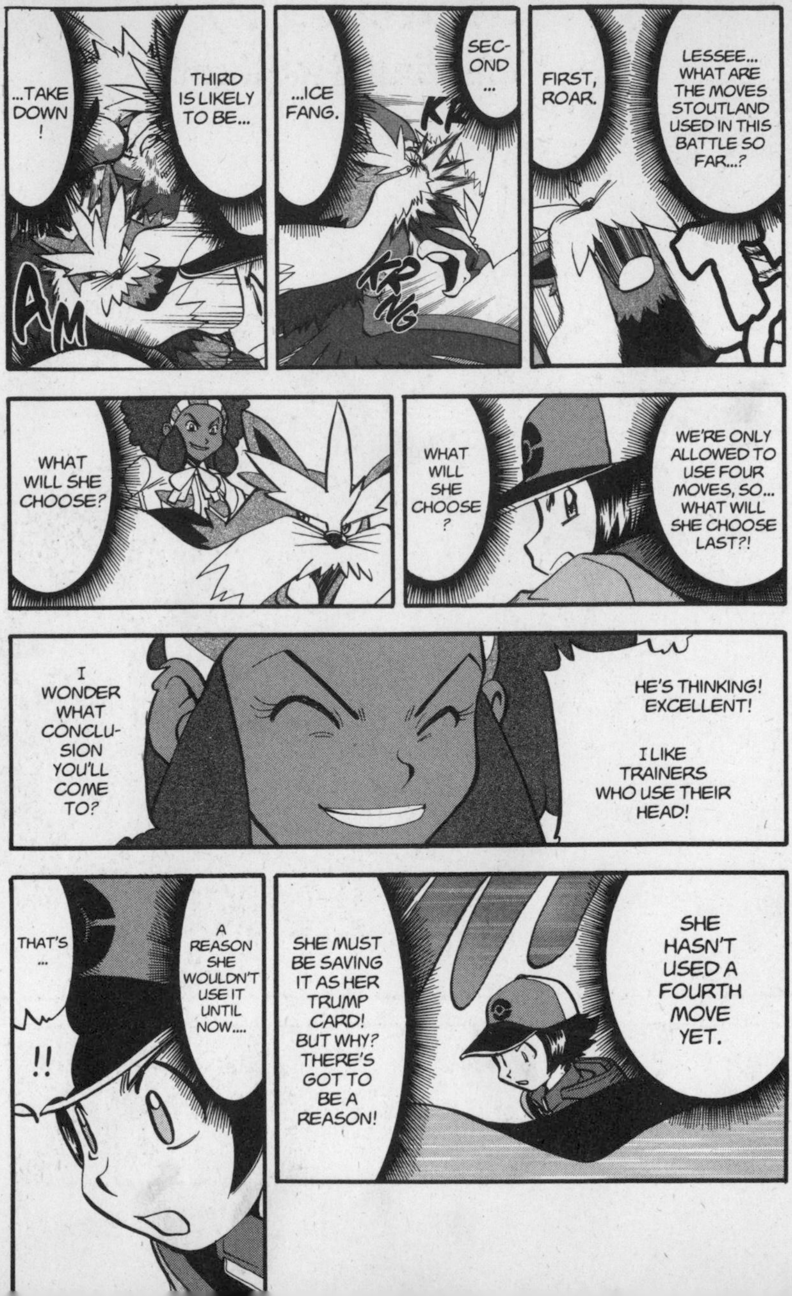
LESSEE... WHAT ARE THE MOVES STOUTLAND USED IN THIS BATTLE SO FAR...?
FIRST, ROAR.
SEC-OND ...
KR
KRNG
...ICE FANG.
THIRD IS LIKELY TO BE...
...TAKE DOWN!
AM
WE'RE ONLY ALLOWED TO USE FOUR MOVES, SO... WHAT WILL SHE CHOOSE LAST?!
WHAT WILL SHE CHOOSE?
WHAT WILL SHE CHOOSE?
HE'S THINKING! EXCELLENT!
I LIKE TRAINERS WHO USE THEIR HEAD!
I WONDER WHAT CONCLU-SION YOU'LL COME TO?
SHE HASN'T USED A FOURTH MOVE YET.
SHE MUST BE SAVING IT AS HER TRUMP CARD! BUT WHY? THERE'S GOT TO BE A REASON!
A REASON SHE WOULDN'T USE IT UNTIL NOW....
THAT'S ...
!!

Adventure 14
Defeating Stoutland

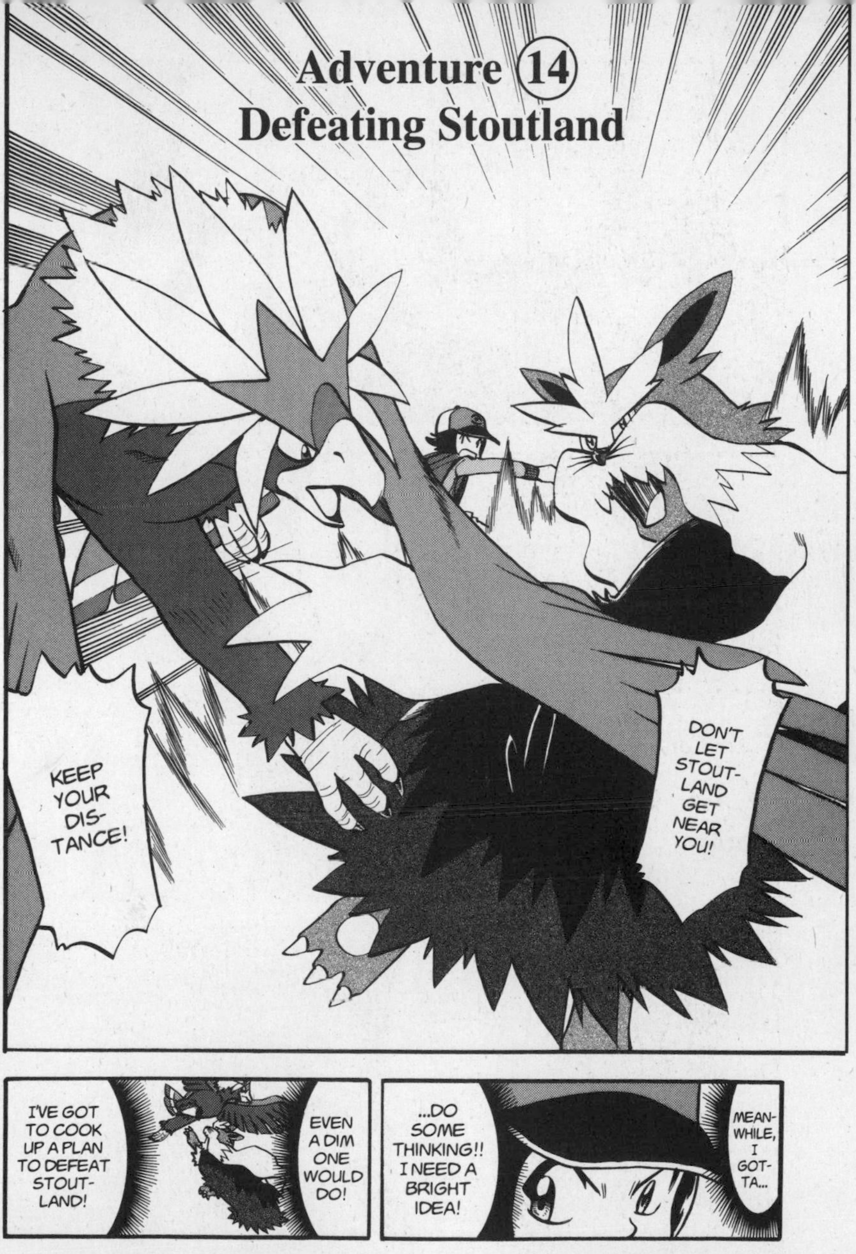
DON'T LET STOUT-LAND GET NEAR YOU!
KEEP YOUR DIS-TANCE!
MEAN-WHILE, I GOT-TA...
...DO SOME THINKING!! I NEED A BRIGHT IDEA!
EVEN A DIM ONE WOULD DO!
I'VE GOT TO COOK UP A PLAN TO DEFEAT STOUT-LAND!

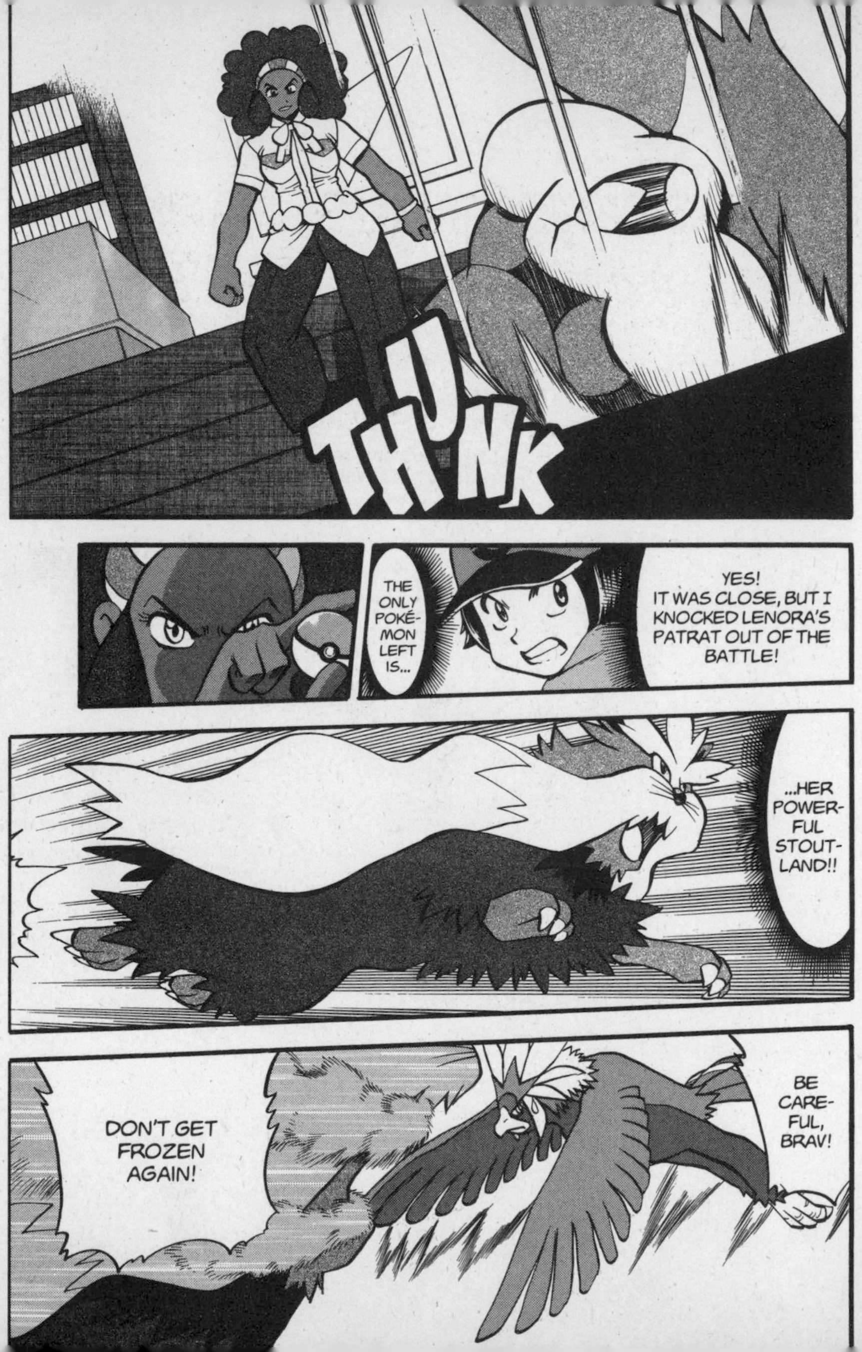
THUNK
THE ONLY POKÉMON LEFT IS...
YES! IT WAS CLOSE, BUT I KNOCKED LENORA'S PATRAT OUT OF THE BATTLE!
...HER POWERFUL STOUTLAND!!
BE CAREFUL, BRAV!
DON'T GET FROZEN AGAIN!

THE STORY THUS FAR!

Pokémon Trainer Black is exploring the mysterious Unova Region with his brand-new Pokédex. Pokémon Trainer White runs a thriving talent agency for performing Pokémon. Now she has hired Black as her assistant. Meanwhile, Team Plasma is plotting to separate Pokémon from their beloved humans...!

BLACK'S dream is to win the Pokémon League!

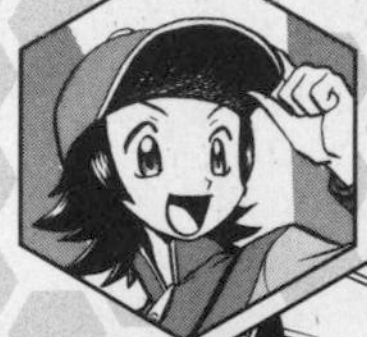

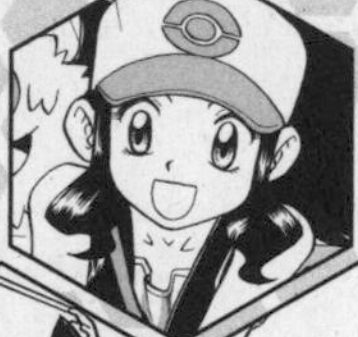

WHITE'S dream is to make her Tepig Gigi a star!

Black's Tepig, TEP, and White's Tepig, GIGI, get along like peanut butter and jelly!

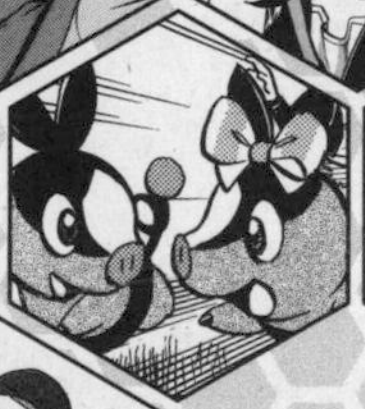

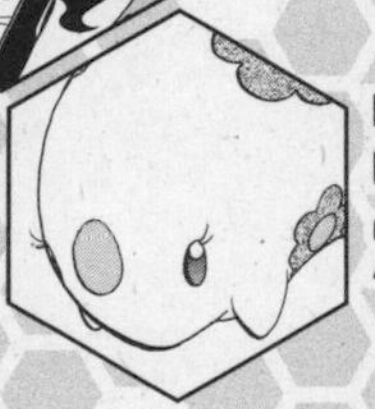

Black's Munna, MUSHA, helps him think clearly by temporarily "eating" his dream.

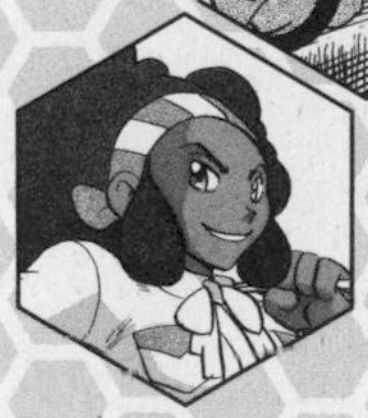

Nicknamed the "archeologist with backbone," LENORA is the Museum Director and Nacrene City Gym Leader.

POKÉMON™

BLACK AND WHITE

VOL. 5

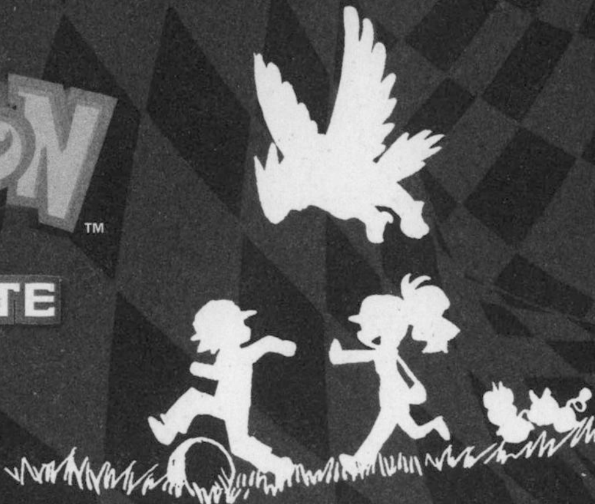

Pokémon Black and White
Volume 5
VIZ Kids Edition

Story by HIDENORI KUSAKA
Art by SATOSHI YAMAMOTO

© 2011 Pokémon.
© 1995-2011 Nintendo/Creatures Inc./GAME FREAK inc.
TM and ® and character names are trademarks of Nintendo.
© 1997 Hidenori KUSAKA and Satoshi YAMAMOTO/Shogakukan
All rights reserved.
Original Japanese edition "POCKET MONSTER SPECIAL"
published by SHOGAKUKAN Inc.

English Adaptation / Annette Roman
Translation / Tetsuichiro Miyaki
Touch-up & Lettering / Susan Daigle-Leach
Design / Fawn Lau
Cover Colorist / Genki Hagata
Editor / Annette Roman

The stories, characters and incidents mentioned in
this publication are entirely fictional.

No portion of this book may be reproduced or transmitted in any form or
by any means without written permission from the copyright holders.

Printed in the U.S.A.

Published by VIZ Media, LLC
P.O. Box 77010
San Francisco, CA 94107

10 9 8 7 6 5 4 3 2 1
First printing, January 2012

www.vizkids.com

www.viz.com

RATED
A
FOR
ALL AGES
PARENTAL ADVISORY
POKÉMON ADVENTURES
is rated A and is suitable
for readers of all ages.
ratings.viz.com

POKÉMON™

BLACK AND WHITE

VOL. 5

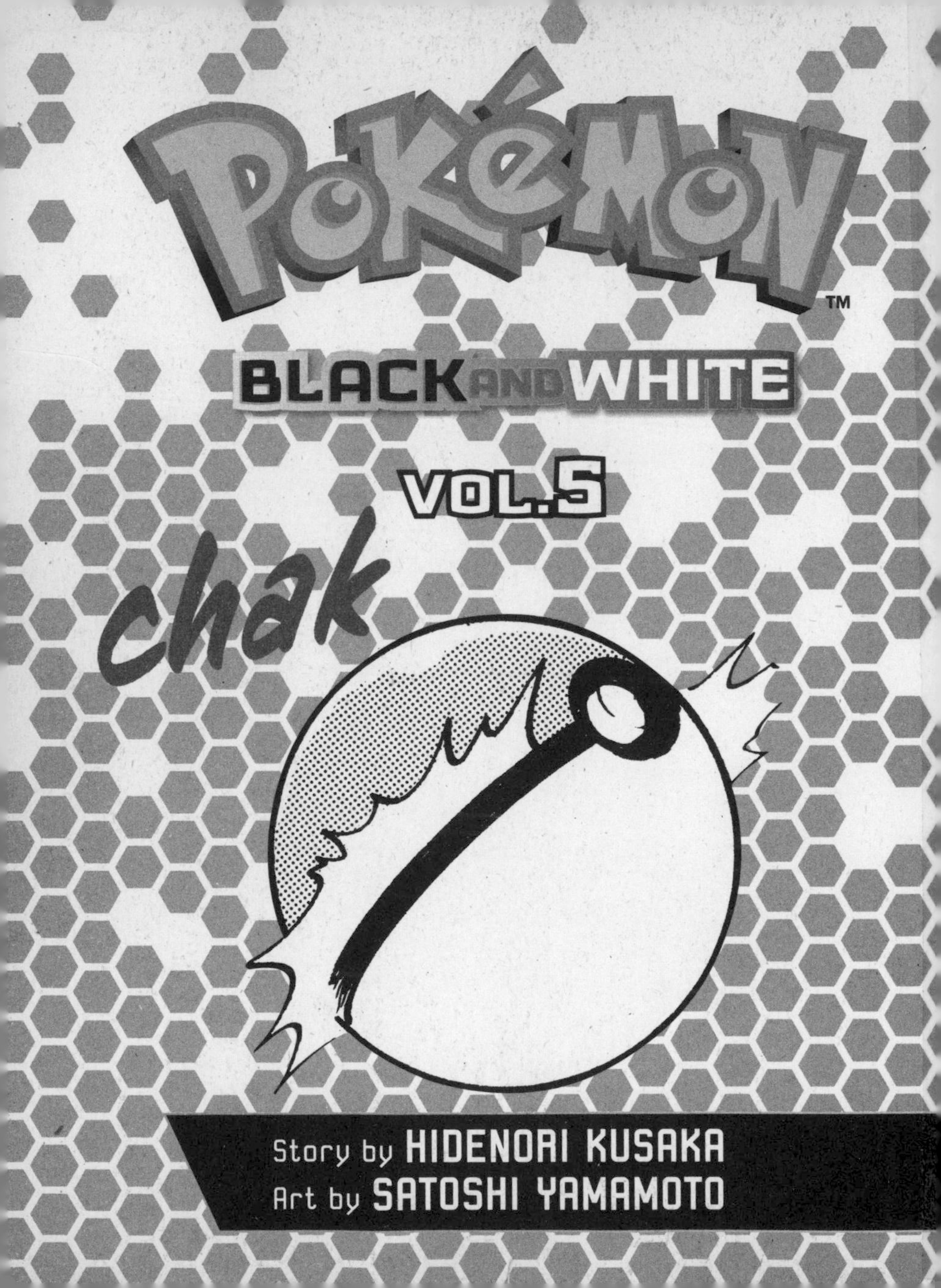
chak

Story by HIDENORI KUSAKA
Art by SATOSHI YAMAMOTO